The
Aftermath

The Aftermath

The Impact Series

C K Westbrook

4 Horsemen
Publications, Inc.

4 Horsemen Publications, Inc.
1497 Main St. Suite 169
Dunedin, FL 34698
4horsemenpublications.com
info@4horsemenpublications.com

Cover and Typesetting by Autumn Skye
Edited by S.L. Vargas

Library of Congress Control Number: 2023947300

Paperback ISBN-13: 979-8-8232-0358-6
Hardback ISBN-13" 979-8-8232-0360-9
EBook ISBN-13: 979-8-8232-0359-3
Audiobook ISBN-13: 979-8-8232-0357-9

For Kristen

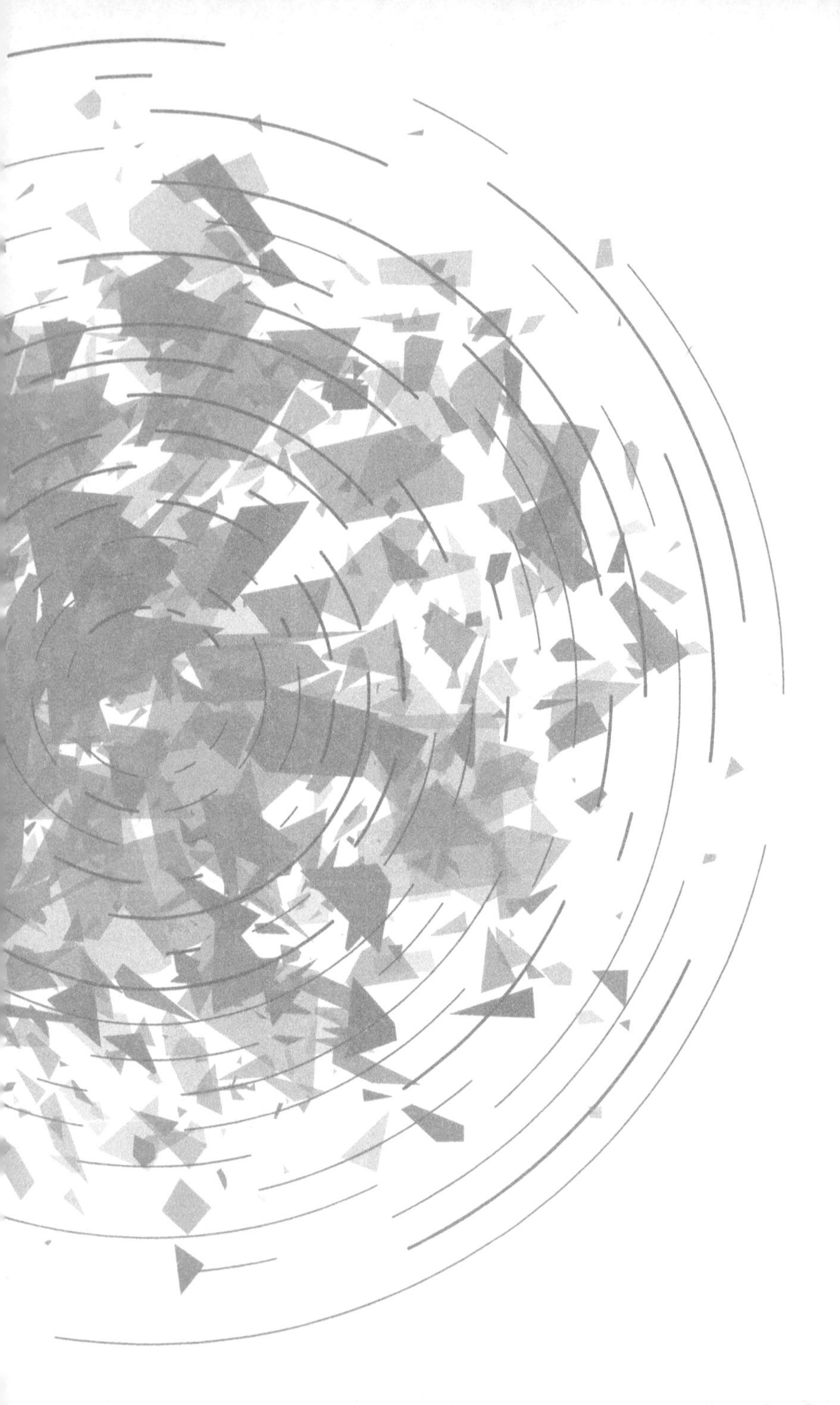

ACKNOWLEDGEMENTS

I must thank 4 Horsemen Publications for their continued support of me and this series. Val, Jen, Erika, and Beau have brought these stories into the world and I am forever grateful. I need to thank Chelsea again for her amazing editing skills, advice, and continued support of me and these books. I want to thank Doreen for her friendship and help in making this story better. Shoutouts to my sisters, Shana and Jess, for their continued assistance, encouragement, and love through this process. As always, I value my silent writing partners, Skye and Bruichladdich, for staying close and being amusing. And once again, I'm forever grateful for Jeffrey, the best decision I ever made. He is always patient, supportive, and there to help me with a kind word or excellent suggestion, he even named this story. And as always, my most profound gratitude is to my readers who have joined me on this adventure. Thank you!

Table of Contents

Prologue

Sixty-Two Days After
the Shooting

<u>Choose to Live in Space, Rather Than Die on Earth Pledge – September 2020</u>

Whereas, I understand that Rex, an extraterrestrial, caused the mass shooting on July 14, 2020, which resulted in hundreds of millions of gun owners turning their weapons on themselves.

Whereas, I understand that Rex caused the mass shooting as punishment because the people of Earth polluted space with debris and garbage and made it unsafe for everyone.

Whereas, Rex asked that the dangerous debris be removed from space or there would be more violence.

Whereas, several individuals, working with NASA and Space Force pulverized all the space debris on September 7, 2020, and made space much safer for everyone.

Whereas, on September 11, 2020, Rex informed the people of Earth that others of his kind were coming and may cause more global violence, despite the clean-up.

Whereas, I understand there MIGHT be an opportunity for Rex to take me into space and spare my life from the pending wrath and violence on Earth.

Whereas, I understand I have a choice to stay on Earth and die or travel into space.

Whereas, I acknowledge and understand that I have no idea, nor does any other human, what living in space will be like. It may be dangerous, scary or even deadly, or fantastic—I have no idea. I only know it will not be like Earth.

Whereas, I choose to go into space with Rex to avoid violence on Earth and I make this decision of my own volition.

In order to go into space with Rex, I pledge to do the following:

I will never use a weapon against my fellow humans or any extraterrestrial;

I will never leave garbage anywhere and will aggressively ensure any waste products caused by my actions, consumption, or work, either directly or indirectly, will be properly and safely recycled or disposed of, or I will not take such action, consumption, or work;

If animals go into space or any are encountered in space, I will not eat them. Since the consumption of animals on Earth caused water pollution, air pollution, habitat destruction, climate change, disease and illness, the biodiversity extinction crisis, and scares and hurts them, out of an abundance of caution and concern all around, I will not eat any animals;

I will always treat my fellow humans and extraterrestrials with kindness and respect, including with justice and equity. I will support diversity and inclusiveness for all, regardless of their species, race, disability, color, religion, planet of origin, sex, or sexual identity;

I will respect and encourage creative and peaceful scientific research, education, and artistic expression;

I will never lie, steal, cheat, or deceive anyone or anything;

I will not be selfish;

I will always reflect on all of my actions and learn about and take into consideration all impacts and consequences to others, including all species, wildlife, and nature, whatever form they take in space;

I will always support a purely democratic government with one human, one vote, and will support free speech;

I take this pledge, not holding any human or extraterrestrial responsible, and assume all personal risk willingly and not under any duress.

Name:

Address:

Email:

If animals can be safe in space and pets are allowed, I would like to bring (pet name/species):

More than 200 million Americans and hundreds of millions worldwide signed The Pledge.

One

One Thousand Eight Hundred and Sixteen Days After the Shooting

Tia slowly walked up the street, gripping the straps of her overstuffed black backpack. She passed rowhouses, some dilapidated and others just plain poor. It was dark, muggy, and quiet except for the occasional car or TV blaring out of an open window. Tia was not judging; she had spent most of her life in houses like these. Poverty was better now since the shooting five years ago. Everyone had healthcare and people looked after one another, but poverty still existed. Memories of growing up in the foster system flashed through her mind. None of her foster parents had money.

This is so stupid, she thought as she pulled a crumpled piece of paper out of her pocket to check that she was on the correct street. The Hill View Hotel was supposed to be somewhere around here but from the looks of the neighborhood, she was not sure she wanted to see it. She continued up the steep street, where the attached row houses morphed into duplexes set back from the road. As she moved farther away from people, the predominant sounds became singing katydids and bat wings flapping as the creatures chased insects above her head. A chubby raccoon, which smelled faintly of watermelon, crossed the street a few hundred feet in front of her and disappeared into the shadows of someone's yard.

She paused to light a cigarette and inhaled deeply, evaluating her next move. She knew vaping was less expensive and easier to find, but she loved old-fashioned cigarettes and relished them when, on very rare occasions, she found some. She took this one from a pack on the front seat of an unlocked car. Since The Pledge, people seldom locked their doors because no one stole anymore—well, almost no one. Tia only took one cigarette from the pack and considered it sharing.

If I keep walking up this hill, I should arrive at the Hill View Hotel. That is what the asshole that stole my cell phone said. It wasn't sharing, because I only had one phone; he stole it.

He said to stay on the main road and walk up and up and up until it ends. I mean, I do love a great view, but Pennsylvania is full of hills and views. What will the view be from the top of this steep hill? Just a dumpy little town.

And why am I doing what a thief said to do?

Tia looked for the moon as she walked up the hill. *Just admit it to yourself, that's not why you're here. Why am I here?*

"Keep up," Tia casually said to a small, fluffy calico cat that followed behind her. Its fur was mostly white with patches of muted orange, tan, and gray. Tia thought she looked like a regular calico cat that had been dipped in bleach, so she called her Clorox.

The cat moved past Tia without giving her a look and proceeded up the steep sidewalk.

Tia squeezed the end of the cigarette to knock out the cherry and save the rest of it for later. She never knew when she could get more.

Suddenly, she was hit in the back so hard that she went down, her forehead cracking against the concrete. Someone landed on her back and the air was knocked out of her lungs.

She gasped.

She struggled to turn her face away from the ground.

She tried to catch her breath but couldn't, not with a large assailant on top of her. She could hear him smelling the back of her head. He grabbed her straight, shoulder-length hair and jerked her head back, inhaling her scent until he wheezed. Tia feared her head would snap off. Warm blood from her forehead dripped down her face.

"Get the fuck off me!" Tia screamed once she had control of her breathing, but with her neck so strained her words came out squeaky rather than forceful.

Panicking, she pushed backward, attempting to headbutt whoever was assaulting her, but the angle was off, and he just jerked out of the way. In the split second that he shifted to her right side, she glanced at him and saw white skin that seemed to glow. His shift to avoid the impact allowed Tia to get her hands to the ground and her knees under her. Suddenly, what felt like a light rain sprinkled upon her shoulders, arms, and head but it burned like acid.

"What the fuck!" Tia screamed. Fueled by a sudden burst of adrenaline, she lurched upward and sent her assailant flying. She looked down at her arms and found what looked like white pieces of plastic burning her flesh. The pain radiated over her back and scalp. She shook her head violently in an attempt to stop the burning. With a scream, she passed out and hit the concrete hard.

Two

Tia snapped up into a sitting position so fast her brain slammed into the front of her skull, or so it felt. She squeezed her eyes shut until the wave of pain passed.

Where am I? Where is the asshole that attacked me? Have I been kidnapped? This shit is not supposed to happen anymore! People are supposed to adhere to The Pledge.

As soon as she could, Tia slowly opened her eyes and looked around the room. She appeared to be in a doctor's office. There was a large window covered with heavy curtains to keep the sun out. The counters were crowded with jars of cotton, injection needles, hand sanitizer, and bandages. But the bed felt too comfortable for a doctor's office and the colorful drapes and carpet did not make sense either.

I think I'm safe, but where is that jerk who attacked me? Did I trip and fall and pass out and have some fucked up concussed nightmare?

Was he smelling my hair?

A flash of the assault seared through her mind. She pulled down the blanket to check out her arms, dotted with little burn marks that were covered in gooey ointment. She pulled her hospital gown up; her hips and thighs were covered with black and blue bruises and her knees were bandaged. Her hands were scraped up and she could feel a tight bandage squeezing her throbbing head.

She slowly got out of bed and walked over to a large full-length mirror to take a look. Beneath the bandages, her eyes were black and blue and her nose had swelled up.

Damn! Looks like I was hit by a truck. What happened to me? Why? Where the fuck am I?

Tia sat back on the bed. A wave of pain started at the top of her head and ran down to her feet. She lay down and squeezed her eyes shut, trying to remember the details of the assault, but it was blurry and so disturbing she decided to think of something nice and beautiful to slow her fast-beating heart, diffuse the pain, and encourage her body to heal.

Very recently, I was staying in a huge, rustic-looking mansion in Deep Creek, Maryland. The house was on a steep hill and overlooked a lake surrounded by a green forest. Each day, I would sit on the deck and watch the sun rise and set. I would watch the colors of the sky change throughout the day. I would watch birds and other creatures go about their lives. It was the most divine place I have ever been in my life.

It wasn't really a crime to squat at the house, which had been left unlocked. The house had solar panels and a battery storage system, so the electricity and air conditioner worked, and the water was on, but the dust and cobwebs gave it a general feeling of abandonment. The day she found it, she picked a small out-of-the-way bedroom and crashed hard on the comfortable bed. She slept there most nights, figuring that even if renters—or the owners—showed up, she could sneak out before they caught her. She locked and blocked the bedroom door and, if needed, she had an escape route out of the window. Planning this way allowed her to sleep more soundly than she had in months.

Her paranoia about safety came from a lifetime of worry in the foster system and it lingered even though there was an enormous reduction in all crime, especially violent crime, since the shooting and The Pledge. Tia knew some news outlets and social media had clocks that counted the days since there had been gun violence in America. There was a big one on-screen in Times Square and another near the White House in D.C. There had not been a single gun-related incident since July 2020.

In the afternoons, she would sneak around and look into the windows of vacation homes occupied by families with kids. The houses seemed chaotic, with kids running in and out to swim, hike, or go on outings. The families seemed so happy and seeing them reminded Tia of the times before the shooting. Not her life, but what she saw in the movies. It was also intriguing to see a baby or toddler since there were so few. There were millions of orphans so few people had biological kids anymore.

With all the energy the families created, she could sense when a house was empty, even with multiple cars parked out front. She would go in and take chips, cookies, sandwich stuff, cereal, clothes, soap, and toilet paper. It wasn't stealing; it was sharing. These people would not miss a few small items; their cupboards and refrigerators were so full, that that food spilled out onto the counters and tables. She even took a few beers sometimes, depending on what she could carry. Since single-use plastic was illegal, the containers were heavier, so she needed to find food every few days. She would fill up the containers and her bag, only taking what she needed. Tia did not mind carrying reusable containers, which in the not-so-distant past would have been considered a great inconvenience. Now no one seemed to mind. She cringed as she thought of all the oil-based plastic waste everyone just cavalierly tossed out before the shooting, including herself.

People were supposed to be less wasteful and only use what they needed, not what they wanted. For the most part, Americans were doing a great job eating organic, vegan food and reducing waste. However, vacations still seemed like an exception to the rules.

Her house was almost three miles off the main road and up a steep hill. She loved the seclusion and safety of knowing she could hear any cars that came up the road, giving her time to move on. No one paid her any attention; they were too busy having fun. If she ran into anyone, she was mistaken for a hiker exploring the trails. She was tall, muscular, and walked with confidence through the woods. She wore shorts, hiking boots, and carried a backpack. She always wore sunglasses.

I found paradise, well until that asshole showed up and stole my phone and told me about the Hill View Hotel. Now, I'm in some weird hospital and I've had the shit beat out of me. As soon as I heal enough, I'm going back. I will find another house. Hell, even if I got caught, what would happen? Since the shooting, people have been kind. Some of them would have probably invited me to dinner after I took food from their cupboards. I mean, it's not like I was violating The Pledge.

"Are you awake?" a woman asked, causing Tia to jump. She opened her eyes, bringing on a new wave of pain. She groaned.

How did I not sense her?

"Well, that is good. We put you on strong pain medication and I was starting to get concerned that you were out too long. How do you feel?" the woman asked.

"Like shit. Like I was hit by a bus. Everything hurts everywhere. What happened? I know someone attacked me but … what the fuck? Was I set on fire?" Tia asked, thinking of the burns that still stung.

"I have no idea what happened. It's strange. You're bruised and banged up like you were hit hard from behind. Your forehead hit the sidewalk. Your thighs and knees are banged up. You have stitches. As if that's not enough, your assailant burned your skin with what seemed like white matches. It's very strange," the woman said. She had a foreign accent that Tia couldn't place.

Tia stared at a pus-filled welt on her arm. *That is no match burn. I'm an occasional smoker and these burns are not from a match. And all these burns happened so fast—almost all at once. This woman is either an idiot or a liar.*

"Where am I? How long have I been here?" Tia asked.

The woman held a thermometer to Tia's head and replied, "You are at the Hill View Hotel, which is no longer a hotel but an educational center here in Janssen. You have been here for almost forty-eight hours. Someone found you unconscious in town and called us to collect you. They thought you were one of us."

She removed the thermometer. "No fever. That's good. Anyway, I'm Doctor Aufseridish and I've been looking after you."

Janssen, yes, that's the name of the town. Shit, forty-eight hours! Where's the cat? Calm down, Tia. Stay calm. Clorox is smart and will know to hide. She is self-sufficient. She is fine. I'm sure she is fine. She had better be fine!

"Thank you for looking after me, Doctor, is it Afidish? I appreciate it. I'm going to lay here a few more minutes and then I'll be on my way," Tia said.

"I think you should stay at least another night. And it's Doctor Aufseridish, like "off-sera-dish," but most people call me Doc. You probably have a concussion. Plus, those burns need to heal. If you were not taking pain medication, they would sting a lot more. I will have some food brought up. Eat. Sleep. Heal. There's no rush," the doctor said.

Tia just nodded and closed her eyes.

The doctor quietly left the room. As soon as the door shut, Tia's eyes shot open, and she slowly sat up.

The doctor did not ask me my name.

She didn't ask where I'm from or why I'm in town or if I need to contact family.

I don't have an ID. The only thing I had on me was that piece of paper with the name and address of this hotel on it, but nope, not a single question about me.

Goosebumps ran up her arms, making the burns sting even more.

This is too strange. I need to get out of here.

Tia couldn't walk out wearing a hospital gown. Where were her clothes?

Moving gingerly, she got out of bed and rummaged around the room, opening drawers and cupboard doors until she found the dirty and bloody clothes she'd had on. Tossing the useless garments in a garbage can marked "biohazardous waste," she continued searching until she found her backpack, which held a couple of reusable containers and clothes, including a pair of tightly rolled hiking pants. She snapped them out and stuck one leg in before another wave of nausea hit and the room started to spin.

Fuck that monster. I think he did give me a concussion.

Tia crumpled to the floor.

She only lay on the floor for a few minutes, too dizzy and weak to get up, before the doctor and another person walked in. The new person was carrying a tray of food that she quickly put down with a loud *clank.* Tia could smell the food and hear the two women speaking but was too dizzy to understand, much less respond.

"Oh dear, help me get her in the bed," the doctor said. They picked Tia up and placed her on the bed. The doctor pulled Tia's pants off.

"Wow, the bruises on her thighs have greatly diminished. I'm going to cut off some of these bandages," she said as she removed the ones from Tia's knees. "These have also faded."

"I wonder who she is? Where she's from?" The other woman asked.

"She is healing fast, but I think her head will need more time," the doctor said as she covered Tia with the blanket. "Leave the food. She might be hungry when she fully wakes up."

The doctor checked her pulse and her eyes.

"She definitely belongs here," the doctor said to the other woman as they walked to the door.

Three

Tia woke up feeling rested. Her head was no longer throbbing and her burns didn't sting. Her stomach growled with hunger. She got out of bed—even her sore muscles felt fine—and stretched her arms up in the air, taking a big breath.

Yep, I feel like my old self again.

She walked over to the window and pulled the long, heavy curtains apart. They were navy blue and light gray and matched the bedding. The sun was still rising and not very bright, but it still triggered a headache. She winced. Through squinty eyes, she took in the well-maintained green lawn. It almost looked like an English garden to her with different tiers, bushes, and flowers. Brightly painted barrels were strategically placed around the grounds, she presumed to collect rainwater. Trees flanked the perimeter where the lawn met the hills in the distance. Even with the window closed, she could smell the grass, dandelions, and buttercups.

The entire scene took her breath away. She thought the other side of the building must have a view of the town.

She moved to the food tray and picked up a yogurt, briefly wondering how long it had sat out and if it might have turned sour before she tore it open and drank it. She knew vegan food did not go bad like food made from animals, but she still wondered sometimes about expiration dates. She had worked in a restaurant for years and knew that bacteria that could make one sick had no discernable smell. She shrugged and put the empty glass container down with a dramatic slam. She opened another glass container with a hummus and vegetable wrap inside.

She ate it in seconds flat.

A bright juicy orange called to her, her body craving the vitamin C. If she ate that, she would be satiated for the entire day and free to leave. She went back to the window and peeled the fruit as she watched the sky grow brighter and change colors; the rising sun's rays reflected off the scattered clouds. She couldn't look away. This time, the light did not hurt her head. She leisurely ate the orange as she watched the sun move across the sky.

With a full stomach, she began to remove her bandages. Her knees, thighs, hips, and hands were almost completely healed; only light greenish bruises remained. The burn marks on her arms were gone, so she imagined it was the same on her head and back. She moved closer to the mirror and began to gently remove the bandage around her head. She was a little puffy and had a grey bruise beneath her eyes, but otherwise looked fine. The doctor mentioned stitches but Tia assumed they had dissolved because she did not see any. Remembering that the back of her head had been burned, she ran her hands through her hair.

Her hair felt strange like there were small bald patches throughout.

"God dammit!" she swore loudly, trying to twist to see the back of her head in the mirror.

Guess I will just look more like a freak than usual. At least my hair grows fast.

Tia ran her fingers through her straight black hair since she did not have a brush. Her hair always wanted to be the same length and color. Even when she dyed it purple and pink as a teenager, it went jet black in just a few days. When she cut it short, it would grow to her shoulders in days. She quit messing with it when she started working, worried people would notice if she changed it and it went back to normal too quickly. People might ask questions she couldn't answer.

Tia quickly dressed and looked around to see if there was anything she could take but she had no interest in medical supplies. She put her hand on the doorknob just as it swung open.

"You're up!" The doctor sounded pleased.

"Yes, thanks, feeling much better. Now I should be on my way. Thank you so much for the care and the breakfast," Tia replied with a smile.

"You healed so fast," the doctor said, touching Tia's chin and looking intensely at her forehead

"Young and healthy," Tia replied, getting nervous as the doctor stared into her eyes. This is why she avoided doctors at all costs. They asked too many questions.

"I guess so," the doctor said, moving past Tia and into the room. "But you should wait. Nafasi, the man that runs this Center, will be here soon to give you a tour. Don't you want to see the Hill View Hotel? It's why you came to Janssen, right? We found the name on a piece of paper in the pocket of your shorts. Here it is," she added, picking up the crumpled paper from the counter near the bandages.

Tia didn't say anything. She didn't trust this woman. She considered rushing out the door and out of the building. But if they wanted to hurt her, they could have while she was unconscious. "What is this place?"

"It's a Center—the Hill View Hotel Center. We are in the medical ward. There are bedrooms, classrooms, conference rooms, a gym, and dining rooms. It was a hotel at one point but it has been renovated. Now it's a research and education center. And it has lovely gardens and grounds and a view, of course. You should take the tour. Learn about what we do here and why," the doctor said. "I think you will find it interesting. I keep forgetting to ask, much to my chagrin, what do they call you here?"

"Tia. Here, there, everywhere," Tia replied, feeling annoyed. "Just tell me now. I can't wait around. I need to be on my way. What kind of research and education do you do here? Is this one of those peaceful commune places? People come here to do yoga and paint rocks and deal with loss and survivors' guilt?"

"I can't tell you. You need to wait for the tour. It's not my place to explain," the doctor said.

"Come on, you're a *doctor*. Just give me the short version," Tia implored, growing more eager to leave but also very curious.

"Can't," the doctor said with a shrug.

"Won't," Tia snapped. She tossed her backpack over her shoulder. "Thanks again, Doc."

Tia swung the door open wide, about to make a break for it, when the doctor said, "But you do belong here, judging by those eyes, that hair, and the way you miraculously healed after that brutal attack. You should stay for the tour."

What was left of the hair on Tia's arms stood up, and adrenaline rushed through her blood. She hustled through the door and down the hall looking for an exit sign and a staircase down to the first floor. Turning down a hall, she came across a wall of elevators. One opened right in front of her.

"Oh hello, Tia," a good-looking man said as he stepped off the elevator. He was well over six feet tall and built like a soccer player. He was so handsome Tia stopped dead in her tracks. He was very tan with auburn, almost red, hair and big blue eyes. The unusual mix made him striking.

She cringed, realizing she was not wearing her sunglasses.

"Oh, you m-m-must be the tour guide," Tia stammered. "I don't have time today. I need to get back. Maybe another time, okay?" She quickly stepped into the elevator he had just vacated.

"Tia, you don't know where you are. Let me at least show you out," the handsome man said, his blue eyes boring into her as he joined her in the now cramped elevator. The doors slid closed, confining them together. She looked at him out of the corner of her eye. He smiled at her in a warm and welcoming way. But she couldn't get over one thing.

How does he know my name?

Four

Tia got out of the elevator at the lobby and quickly bounded toward the door. She did not say goodbye to the hot tour guide, just left him in the elevator. She did not need help finding her way out or back to town.

As soon as she exited the building, she was almost blinded by beauty. In the morning sunlight, the sky was streaked with many colors and the grass appeared wet and verdant. Birds flew about and she could hear their wings beating. She inhaled deeply and smelled recently cut grass, pine trees, and many other organic scents, including fruits, vegetables, and flowers.

There must be a garden nearby.

Tia took a few more loud, deep breaths. She could hear doves, robins, and sparrows singing and bickering.

"It's beautiful, isn't it? Everything here is so magnificent. Please, Tia, let me show you around. I know you will enjoy it," the handsome man said, jolting her out of her thoughts.

This place is sensory overload.

It was very rare for someone to sneak up on her with her sensitive hearing.

"Come on, thirty minutes is all I ask, and you can be on your way if you'd like," he urged.

"Okay," Tia said with a shrug, hoping the garden was on the tour. "Whatever."

I'm heading to town to find Clorox immediately afterward.

"Great! This building has a medical center, as you know. Just a few rooms on the third floor for the doctor and occasional patient, and some labs for research. It's not a hospital by any stretch and this building is multi-purpose. Other floors have offices and conference rooms. The hotel reception and the dining rooms and kitchens are behind this building, in the main building. But look at the architecture. This building was constructed in the early 20th century. The main building is even more lovely. Come, walk this way," he said enthusiastically.

As Tia walked, she rummaged in her backpack until she found her sunglasses. She quickly put them on before he looked at her again; she preferred to conceal her eyes from people she did not know.

"I assume the doc told you I'm Nafasi Genny and this is my Center. We have 28 guests here now and 24 staff including the doctor and her assistant, the nurse. We reflect on the shooting and what it means to us, how it has impacted our lives, and what it means moving forward," Nafasi explained as he walked. "We also talk about the pandemic, how it impacted people's lives, how it started by abusing and torturing animals, and how we—as individuals and as a society—must ensure we don't have another pandemic."

"You know the lab leak theory has not been officially disproven," Tia said.

He paused and looked Tia in the eyes. "We know Ebola, MERS, mad cow disease, West Nile, HIV, H1N1, and SARS are diseases that spread to humans due to our treatment of animals, be it unethical hunting; horrible living conditions in factory farms and live animal wet markets; feeding cows to cows; mixing species that should never be near each other; and caging them in cruel ways that make them scared and sick. When immune systems weaken, viruses jump from animal to animal and species to species. Plus, humans destroy the animals' habitats, making people, species, and viruses come together more often. Whether the lab was working with the virus or not, it originated in nature. Human's terrible behavior caused the pandemic. But not anymore. We are all better behaved now. We treat nature with respect. We are mostly vegan and we help people embrace this new and kind way of living. We help people enjoy this new beautiful, loving world."

I was right. Another one of those communes that popped up over the past five years.

Everyone had a different reaction to the world-wide mass shooting that killed hundreds of millions of people in fifteen minutes. Tia could understand the purpose of a center like this to help people with their emotional trauma in the aftermath. Hell, she had signed The Pledge and held her breath waiting to see what would kill them next, just like almost everyone else. Her heart pounded as she remembered how stressful it was. The world had not even dealt with the chaos from the shooting before everyone had looked up at the words "they're here," written in the clouds.

The world watched that terrifying cloud for almost fifteen hours, waiting for the aliens' judgment.

That event, like the pandemic and shooting, changed the world forever. Humanity got to sit with its fear. Reflect on its behavior. Be judged for its choices, and make a public commitment to be better. Of course, those who lost parents, kids, and friends in the worldwide mass shooting suffered the most emotional trauma.

I never felt the need or desire to come to one of these places, but if people get closure or peace here, I'm fine with that. Though I do hope it's not a cult. Those have popped up a lot as well.

"And we must ensure we never have another mass shooting. Rex came because of the deadly pollution that caused the collision that killed his parents. If it had not been for Kate Stellute and Sinclair Jones, every one of us may have been punished by Rex's colleagues, the mysterious 'others.' We all promised to not be wasteful, violent, or cruel to prevent Rex and the others from causing more violence. My attacker violated The Pledge," Tia fumed.

Nafasi looked at her but did not acknowledge her words. He walked out onto the lawn, indicating that Tia should follow. "You can see the solar panels from this angle." He pointed up. "We have a few battery walls and we have electric heat pumps. We converted natural gas heating to geothermal. We collect and clean the rainwater to supplement our well." He nodded at a brown wooden cistern near a tall ledge. "Luckily, Pennsylvania still gets plenty of rain. And up here, we are spared the terrible flooding. It would've been better if we'd just lived sustainably all along, you know, before The Pledge. It is easy. Once the conversions are done, you don't even have to think about it. And we feel more at peace with nature."

Tia just nodded.

As they walked across the manicured lawn, the grass and shrubs gave way to trees and paths. Nafasi led her down an unmarked path.

"We are vegetarian and vegan here, of course, and have a spectacular garden I want to show you. We raise chickens for eggs and have a few goats and sheep for milk. They also maintain the lawns. Don't they do a fantastic job? It almost looks mowed," Nafasi continued.

Walking alongside him, Tia nodded.

"See, isn't it lovely!" Nafasi said, expanding his arms as they turned a corner and the garden came into view.

It had vegetable rows, fruit trees, flowers, berries, herbs, and other things Tia could not immediately identify by sight or smell. Bees and other insects buzzed. She spotted a bright yellow American Goldfinch flying overhead. Even the tall chain-link fence around it did not diminish its beauty.

The garden soothed Tia, making her feel less restless and eager to leave.

"Yes, it's very nice. As a city girl, I grew up getting most of my food at a 7-11 or fast-food restaurant. I ate a lot of meat without thinking about where it came from. Hell, I worked at a fast-food restaurant for a few years. This is amazing. I guess it's a lot of work?" Tia stared at the garden, in awe of their ability to produce food so close to where they lived.

This guy is nice and the doctor was helpful. In some ways, the guy who stole my cell phone was right about this place. He said it was beautiful. Of course, he also said there would be no one here.

"We all work together and we all spend time in the gardens. It's a labor of love. We also work with nature. See those fields down there? Those are sunflowers. We feed the birds and other animals so they stay away from the garden. We act like we don't want them there, and have scarecrows, noise, and other natural deflectors. We make them work for their seeds, way over there. So far, it has been working well. Come, I will show you the main building next," he said, leading Tia down a different path back toward the buildings.

"I guess you still need to go to stores and eat some corporate food. Can that garden feed fifty-plus people? And what do you do in the winter? Despite climate change, Pennsylvania still gets snow in the winter," Tia said as they passed some goats and sheep, chomping on grass. She spotted chicken coops off in the distance. She loved the smell of animals and farms.

Nafasi turned to look at her with an odd expression. "We have a greenhouse as well. The food we grow sustains us. We don't eat much, just like you."

What does he mean by that? How does he know how much I eat?

Tia walked faster, once again eager to end the tour and leave.

"And here is the main building," Nafasi said, nodding toward an elegant structure. "It was built in 1908 in the neoclassical style, what with the columns and marble porch. Look at all the detail in the eaves and roof. See the animals and gargoyles? Kind of a crazy mix of styles, but it sure does work. The landscape manager lights it up at night depending on the season or what he is in the mood for—he is very creative. I just love this building. It takes a lot of upkeep, but it's worth it. Inside is the main kitchen, dining hall, conference rooms, ballrooms, and the guestrooms where most staff and guests stay. The lobby is dazzling. The swimming pool and flower gardens are behind the building. Come, I will show you the hedges and pine gardens."

Tia spotted the road leading down the hill and felt a sense of urgency to leave this place, which was too perfect.

Definitely a cult. This is how they get you.

"I need to get going. Thank you for the tour and for allowing the doctor to take care of me. I can't thank you enough." Tia pulled her backpack over both shoulders and straightened her back.

"You must see the view! You can't leave until you see why such a spectacular place has such a simple name. The Hill View Hotel Center lives up to its name, I promise! Come, it will just take a couple of minutes. It will take your breath away," Nafasi cajoled.

He gently took her elbow and guided Tia through the front door. The stunning lobby had floor-to-ceiling windows, and white marble floors covered with funky rugs that made the room seem both sterile and inviting. Bookshelves covered the opposite wall and lush plants gave it a delicious, earthy smell. The antique reception desk was made of dark shiny wood and looked like something from the last century. The ceiling was painted like a church, with people, clouds, animals, suns, moons, and planets. Tia stumbled as she looked up and around.

Nafasi led her down a hall to some elevators and hit the button to go up. "This building has seven floors. The top few have good views, but the roof garden has the best."

They got out of the elevator on the seventh floor and walked up a steep spiral staircase made of stone. Nafasi pushed open a modern-looking door—a harsh contrast to the old-looking staircase—onto the roof. Tia was greeted by the overwhelming smell of mulch and fertilizer as she looked around at the pots of flowers, small trees, and shrubs everywhere. Long boxes with spinach, tomatoes, kale, herbs, and other plants grew healthy and strong.

"The government has recommended that all roofs without solar panels have a garden. We have enough room for both. See, more food," Nafasi said pointing at a pot of kale. "But *this* is what I really wanted to show you."

The view was so stunning it almost hurt Tia's eyes. Green rolling hills went on for miles until they bumped into white fluffy clouds. The sun was still climbing up into the sky. She could see a winding river off in the distance and forests of green spruce trees. Tia could see the town way down the hill. From here, it almost looked quaint, with its row houses, a few buildings, and churches. She could not see the chipped paint and broken windows, nor that the churches and many buildings were vacant.

"What do you think?" Nafasi asked.

Tia nodded her head and smiled. "That is a nice view. The green, blue, and orange are stunning. Tree-covered hills always look like heads of broccoli to me from this distance. And you can't tell the town is poor and beaten down," Tia replied. "It looks quaint, almost pretty from way up here."

"Yes, big gun-owning community. It lost like 70% of its citizens in the mass shooting. The ones that stayed are very depressed and haven't managed to get it together yet. Most are still surviving day by day," Nafasi said.

Tia wondered why his Center did not do more to help the town but figured it was none of her business.

"Is there a lot of crime? That seems odd, especially with the low violent crime rate nowadays." She squinted in an attempt to see if she could locate the general area where she was attacked.

"As I said, it's a depressed community. Depression can lead to drug use. Maybe your assailant was on drugs since the attack was so violent. There's not a lot of crime but it still happens sometimes. I'm sorry that it happened to you," Nafasi said, looking at Tia.

He was so handsome and he looked into her eyes with such intense compassion that she had to look away.

"Who brought me here?" Tia asked, turning her attention back to the view. "The doc said someone found me."

"A local was walking their dog and saw you on the sidewalk near the road that leads up here. They didn't recognize you and figured you were heading here, so they called and Brenda and Wai went down to see what was up. When they saw you had been assaulted and were bleeding badly, they rushed you up to see the doc. Were you robbed? Doc said you had nothing with you but some clothes—no ID, money, or even a phone. What exactly did they take?" he asked.

Nothing. I had nothing to steal. They didn't even take my backpack, which contained a lighter, a couple of books borrowed from the mansion, a water bottle, reusable food containers, some clothes, and sunglasses. Maybe it was some crazed salt bath meth-type attack, but it was not a robbery.

"Are there police in the town?" Tia asked, without addressing his question.

"No. I think there are some in the next town over. I have never encountered any here. I got this Center going after the shooting, so there were only a few police officers anywhere in rural Pennsylvania by then. Do you want us to reach out and find some? We can do that. Might take a few days," Nafasi said.

"No. Not necessary. If it *was* a crazed junkie, it's best to just avoid them. I will be leaving town soon—out before it gets dark. But thanks for the offer," Tia said, as she started to walk toward the door.

I don't want any more attention on me. The guy who stole my phone was right: this place is exquisite and a delightful sensory overload. I wish I could stay, but he led me to believe it was empty, like my Deep Creek mansion. I'm an idiot for believing a thief.

Tia's heart skipped a beat and she got goosebumps everywhere.

Nafasi just said I had nothing on me, so he discussed my situation with the doctor. How did he know my name at the elevator? I had only told the doc a moment earlier. What the fuck is going on?

"Thanks again for the tour and the medical care but I need to leave. I want to be out of town before dark," Tia said before a flash of movement, the color of orange, caught her eye. "Is that a tiger?" she asked incredulously, not believing her own eyes. In the distance, where the lawn became a forest, she thought she spotted an enormous cat.

Nafasi quickly walked away and returned seconds later with binoculars. "We have these all over for bird watching. Feel free to use them," he mumbled as he scanned the grounds. "Yes, there it is. It's a tiger. Take a look," he said, handing the binoculars to Tia.

"Holy shit, it is," Tia said as she focused on the huge cat. "Why is it here?"

"There used to be thousands of cruel roadside zoos all over America. The shitty owners and managers carried guns so many shot themselves. The animals were left to starve, dehydrate, and die because Americans focused on *human* needs first. But eventually, people realized a lot of people died at those roadside houses of horror and stepped in to help the animals. We have a lot of property here so I took in some tigers and other abandoned exotics. Luckily, wildlife trade and exotic pet ownership have been outlawed, but someone needs to clean up the mess of those animal abusers. I believe keeping an animal in a cage is torture," Nafasi said.

"I agree, but to have wild animals roaming around? What do they eat?" Tia asked, watching the cat settle under a tree. It looked a little old and beat up.

"Deer. Gophers. Nature has rebounded here and they play the role of top predator. We do provide some food with the necessary vitamins because their hunting skills aren't great. These cats were born in captivity, but it is best to avoid them. A veterinarian came with them and helped us get everything set up. All the exotics have been spayed and neutered. I wanted an elephant, but it didn't work out."

Knowing there were tigers (*plural*) roaming around made Tia even more eager to get down the hill and out of town while there was still daylight. She did not want to know what other exotics were living in the forest. And she was worried they might have found her cat, Clorox.

"Thanks again for everything, but I need to go," Tia said, handing back the binoculars and walking quickly to the door. Nafasi followed her down the stairs.

I'm out of here. This guy knew my name. I think the doctor is lying. And I need to find Clorox.

When Tia got to the elevator, she pressed the down button and waited. To fill the silence she added, "This place is lovely and the view is spectacular—so vibrant. Thank you for showing me."

"I thought you would see it like that, the way we do," Nafasi said.

"What do you mean?" Tia asked as the elevator doors opened. With her attention on Nafasi, she didn't see the man waiting for her inside.

He pressed a cloth against Tia's nose and mouth, cutting off her ability to breathe. She jerked her head away, inhaling sharply to scream. Instead, she inhaled the chemical fumes and passed out into Nafasi's arms.

Five

Tia woke up in the same room as before.

What the fuck happened?

It was dark. A small lamp provided little light, and the curtains were pulled shut. Her head throbbed.

Angry and confused, she struggled to remember why she was there. *I had a tour of the grounds and the gardens. A spectacular view. Was it a dream?* Tia dragged herself up and looked around for her backpack, relieved to find it. *Why am I here? I was attacked and I healed, right? And left, I think.*

Tia found her clothes and got dressed. Her sunglasses were at the bottom of the bag.

Did I get dressed before? Was there a tour? Or was that a dream? My head hurts. I'm sure I was attacked. Burned. Did the doctor say I had a concussion? Maybe I should just lie down. Doc is nice. There was food and I healed fast. I'm fine. I think. This bed is comfortable. It's not a hospital bed, more like a hotel room....

Tia fell asleep.

Six

Tia had a nightmare. It was late, and she roamed the dark streets of the shabby town. It was strangely and eerily quiet, with no insects, owls or flapping bat wings to be heard. She searched for Clorox while dodging violent drug addicts and tigers. Her heart raced.

She jerked awake, certain that someone had called to her.

What was that?

A bird cawed loudly outside the window. Tia jumped out of bed and pulled back the curtains. It was early afternoon, and several large black crows were flying about and making a racket.

Her head throbbed and she rubbed her temple.

Suddenly, the door swung open. Tia jumped.

"You're finally awake!" the doctor said pleasantly. "I brought food. You must be hungry. Here, tofu and veg sandwich, apple, and juice."

She placed the food on the counter and walked over to Tia. She lightly touched her chin and looked into her eyes. "How is your head?"

"What happened?" Tia asked. "I'm so confused."

"How is your head? How do you feel?" the doctor asked again, her brow furrowed.

"Okay, I guess. A mild headache," Tia replied.

"Sit down and eat and hydrate. That will help a lot," the doctor said.

Tia drank the juice in one long gulp. She devoured the sandwich and reached for a glass of water the doctor had filled for her.

"You were assaulted in town. The staff brought you here, to the Hill View Hotel Center. We think it was a drug addict that robbed you. He slammed you into the ground and gave you a concussion. You felt better and were getting a tour of the garden when you collapsed. You were brought back here. Your head injury was worse than I thought. You need rest. I'm going to insist you stay a couple of days until we are sure you will not faint again. Luckily, Naf was there to catch you before you hit your head again," the doctor explained.

Who is Naf? Why am I at the Hill View Hotel Center? And why am I so tired? Everything is so muddled.

"What's your name again?" Tia asked.

"Doctor Brigit Aufseridish. Off-sera-dish. It's a mouthful. You, and many others, just call me Doc," she explained.

"Oh, right," Tia said, acting as though she remembered. "And what is Naf?"

"Naf is short for Nafasi Genny. This is his Center, and he was giving you a tour when you fainted. Just lay down. Sleep is the best medicine now. When you wake up, I'm sure you will feel better," Dr. Aufseridish said as she helped her lay back and pulled the blanket over her.

"Where are you from? What is that accent?" Tia asked. "Sorry if I already asked."

"Israel. I'm Jewish and an Israeli citizen. I moved here three years ago," Dr. Aufseridish responded.

"Did you come to help us after the mass shooting? Or did Israel get hit so hard you had to leave?" Tia asked, trying to stay focused and awake. Tia did not follow international news but she was curious about how other countries were impacted.

"We only lost ten percent of our population on July 14, 2020, less than a million people. I say 'only' because the statistic is incomparable to the United States. America lost more than seventy million—over twenty percent—of its people."

"Did you come here to help us?" Tia asked.

"Yes, I came here to help you, and to help Nafasi," Dr. Aufseridish replied.

"How long have I been here? When was I mugged?" Tia asked. She was struggling to follow the conversation and stay awake.

"About forty-eight hours ago. Get some sleep," the doctor added as she pulled the curtains closed and walked out of the room.

Two days? Shit, I need to find Clorox. After a quick nap, I will go find her.

Seven

Tia tossed and turned, dreaming about Clorox. The cat screamed at her to get up and find her. She woke, breathless and sweaty.

Oh shit, I'm still in this hotel-hospital room. I need to go. I need to find Clorox. Something weird is going on.

Tia rummaged through the cabinets until she found a toothbrush and soap. She quickly cleaned up and got dressed. She could not find a brush again, but her hair always looked poker-straight anyway. She wondered if it still had small bald patches from the burns but couldn't bring herself to touch it.

The doctor said I was burned with matches but that is not true.

She did not look out the window because she did not care what time it was, she was leaving now. She grabbed her backpack, put on the sunglasses, and reached for the doorknob. It was locked.

What the fuck?

She felt a moment of panic, but then the door swung open.

"Hi, Tia. How are you feeling? I'm Brenda, Dr. Aufseridish's nurse and I have some dinner for you. I will just put it over here." She placed some metal and glass containers on the counter. "Doc said you should hydrate to help with the headache. Here's some water and juice made from apples grown on the property."

"The headache is gone. I feel fine. But I will drink this juice, thanks," Tia said before gulping it down. "Delicious, thanks. I'm not hungry and I need to go."

"Well, I'm sure Doc will want to see you before you go. Make sure you're okay," Brenda said. "She will be here shortly, so why don't you have a seat, eat, and just wait for a few."

"Sorry, I'm in a rush," Tia said, heading toward the door.

"I guess it's okay. You do look so much better than when we found you on the street," Brenda said.

Tia turned to face Brenda. "You found me?"

"Yep, Wai Xing and I were working here, in the medical ward, when a local called and said she found a seriously injured woman on a sidewalk that seemed to be heading up our hill and could we help. Wai and I rushed right down and found you," Brenda explained. "You were unconscious, bloody, and had a serious head injury. But you were breathing and seemed okay to move. Your arms were burnt and there were matches scattered around. Thank God the nut bag that assaulted you didn't set you on fire!"

Why would someone burn me with matches? Why is everything so fuzzy?

"I mean, I'm generally very patient and understanding when it comes to drug addiction and PTSD, but violence is uncalled for," Brenda continued.

Didn't the doctor and I discuss this? Yes, Doc said they were match burns. I don't think it was matches, though.

"And to attack a person from behind and leave them to die in the street? Well, that is barbaric. And strange. I have not seen or heard of that kind of random violence since I moved here three years ago. It's disturbing. I'm so sorry that happened to you."

Tia sat down on the bed; she wanted to hear more. "What position was I found in?"

"On your stomach. It looked like you had been hit very hard from behind. We rushed you right up here to Doc. She must have used some powerful medication because you look great. No swelling or bruising. Of course, you do have a concussion—you fainted with Nafasi so maybe you heal faster on the outside than the inside."

"What time did you find me?" Tia asked.

"Around 9:30. It only took us a few minutes to drive down the hill," Brenda replied.

"Was the person that called still with me when you arrived? Had they seen what happened?" Tia asked.

"No, they were gone. They gave us a good description of where to find you so we were there quickly."

"Huh, was it a man or woman that called? Did they speak to you or Wai Xing? Did the person have your cell number? Or did they call someone else first?" Tia questioned.

Dr. Aufseridish walked in before Brenda could respond.

"Hi, Doc. I'm filling in some gaps for the patient on what happened. Tia, I'm a nurse, not a detective. I'm not sure who called or how they got to me, I'm just happy they did. And like I said, violent assaults are rare so we just kind of jumped into action to get to you. You are healing well so I think we should all just be happy it did not end worse," Brenda said with a kind smile.

"Yes, good point. I mean, maybe we should try to catch this asshole, you know, before he hurts someone else," Tia said, miffed. She was annoyed no one seemed intent on finding her assailant.

"Yes, maybe we should find a police officer and report this incident," Dr. Aufseridish said. "We should discuss this with Nafasi and help find the assailant."

Whoops. What am I thinking? No cops. Now I'm making this more complicated. I need to leave. I need to find the cat and get back to Deep Creek. Or just away from people.

"Oh, now I recall there are no cops here. I discussed that with someone. My memory seems messed up right now. Oh well, probably for the best. I don't want to start trouble with the locals. I'm just passing through anyway. Thanks again for all your help," Tia stood and started for the door.

"If your memory is giving you trouble maybe you should stay another night. Concussions are very serious," Dr. Aufseridish added.

Tia rested her hand on the doorknob but hesitated. "When did you get me, Brenda? When did you find me on the sidewalk?"

"Like I said, around 9:30. You sure do heal fast. It's quite extraordinary," Brenda replied, looking intently into Tia's eyes.

Tia winced. She needed to get away fast before Brenda started to ask questions about her eyes. "No, I mean how long have I been here, at the Center, in this medical room, since you found me on the sidewalk?"

"I guess we picked you up around forty-eight hours ago," Brenda replied.

Wait? What? That doesn't make sense, Tia thought just before the room went black.

Eight

Someone or something was on her back, crushing her into the concrete and sniffing the back of her head, hair, and neck. He grabbed her hair, pulling her head back. She felt like he was going to bite her and it filled her with pure terror. She glimpsed a white blur out of the corner of her eye. He looked like a pale human with a bizarre-shaped mouth. Or a black hole where a mouth should be. She wanted to scream but was suddenly lit on fire.

Tia pulled herself awake from the nightmare.

This feels like déjà vu or Groundhog Day but whatever it is, it's over now.

She quietly tried to open the door and was not surprised to find it locked.

Every time I try to open this door someone comes in. It's too much of a coincidence. Are they waiting on the other side?

She went to the window and pulled it open. As she inhaled the fresh night air, her mind felt less fuzzy and some clear memories of her tour came back to her. She thought she heard a noise, somewhere far off. It was faint, like an alarm going off in town.

Thank God Nafasi loves historic architecture and left the old-fashioned windows, the kind that actually open, Tia thought as she knocked out the screen. She slid out of the window and sat on the windowsill, her legs still in the room. She recalled from the tour that she was three floors up. She hoped there was grass below her and not marble. She knew she could survive a three-floor jump, well, she could, *depending* on what she landed on. She was scared and desperate and needed to jump, so why look down?

She tugged her backpack tight, pulled her legs through the window, turned her torso around, and thrust herself off the sill and into the darkness. She hit the ground with a painful grunt and her legs buckled beneath her. Grass. She landed on the grass.

As soon as she could, she got up and staggered toward the front of the building and to the road that led down the hill. There was only a sliver of a moon so it was dark. With each step, she felt better and she quickened her pace. She tried to stay as far as she could from the road, walking close to the tree line so she could duck behind them in case a car came up or down the hill. The faint alarm sound had stopped. The air was full of soothing night sounds, croaking frogs, and cricket songs. Fireflies seemed to be leading her down the hill.

I love how quickly nature has rebounded.

Barely anyone talked about the biodiversity extinction crisis anymore. It had been all gloom and doom and the end of all civilization when she was growing up. Ocean acidification would lead to food web collapse and mass human starvation. Eight billion people were killing and eating everything in sight. But since the shooting and The Pledge, nature has been allowed to recover and thrive.

Of course, it's impolite to discuss the good that came from the global mass shooting and pandemic, but I don't give a shit. In many ways, the world is so much better.

A high-pitched terrifying yowl stopped Tia dead in her tracks. Fearing she had been spotted, she sprinted into the shadow of a tree and crouched down.

Another yowl filled the night air but this time Tia shot up.

"Clorox!" Tia shouted into the darkness. "Where are you?"

Tia's heart raced. She hoped it was Clorox, as she had never heard the cat make that noise before. She was also afraid of why the cat was making such a ter-rifying sound.

Tia frantically searched around the trees, wan-dering farther away from the road. Without a phone or flashlight, it was very difficult to see. She called out many times but heard nothing except other creatures going about their lives.

Fuck, there are tigers out here! Am I notifying them I am here? Would they come this close to the road?

Tia was torn between alerting predators to her location and her need to find Clorox.

"If you can make a sound, I might be able to find you. Otherwise, I'm going to sit down right here and wait for daylight, and then I will find you. I promise. I'm sorry. It's too dark. Hell, I'm afraid I might step on you!" Tia whispered loudly into the darkness. An owl hooted several times, as though agitated that Tia was in its territory.

Tia was tired, worried, and frustrated but still managed to doze off at some point.

Not long after, a loud bird call startled Tia awake. She had fallen asleep leaning against a tree. It was still dark, but she could see a glimmer of light on the horizon. It was getting lighter and soon she could properly search for Clorox.

She stood up and stretched. "Clorox, please make a sound if you can?"

Despite the silence, Tia started searching, her eyes scanning the ground, looking at the base of trees and shrubs and rocks. As it grew lighter, she could see farther distances.

And then she saw it, 200 feet away, against some tree roots: a splash of white and gray against all the green and brown.

Tia ran to her, "Oh Clorox, I'm so relieved to see you!" She squatted down beside her.

Tia gasped in horror. The small cat looked emaciated. Her fluffy hair was missing in spots, exposing her wrinkled pink cat skin, which was covered with bits of plastic and burn welts. Clorox opened her green eyes and looked at Tia. There was recognition, but also resignation. Clorox was dying.

"No, no, no," Tia repeated as she gently picked her up and walked as quickly as she could back up the hill. "You are the toughest, most independent, and most confident cat I have ever known. How did you fall apart this badly—and so quickly? I see the horrible burns, yes, but how are you starving and dehydrated after three days? Okay, you walked up here, like a mile, with severe burns. Maybe that emaciated you?

It doesn't make sense," Tia mumbled to the cat in a soothing voice, gently hugging the cat to her chest.

She could see the Hill View Hotel lit by the early morning sunshine and wished she could run to the doctor. Suddenly, a thought struck her that made her blood run cold.

It wasn't forty-eight hours plus last night. They kept saying forty-eight hours. Today would be my third day, according to the doctor and Brenda. How fucking long have I been here?

Every fiber in Tia's being told her to turn around and get out of that town but instead, she started to run to the Center.

"Hang on, Clorox. They have medicine. You will feel better soon. Just hang on!" Tia whispered to the half-dead cat.

Nine

By the time she pushed open the front door to the building that contained the medical offices, Tia was sweating and panting. She rushed to the elevator and pushed the button to the third floor, mumbling, "Come on, come on" under her breath until it opened.

Finally, she reached her floor. As she turned down the hall where she thought her room was, she stopped dead in shock. Brenda was sitting outside of her room, reading a newspaper, a cup of coffee on the floor by her chair.

"What the hell!" Brenda exclaimed, kicking over the coffee in her rush to stand up. The sound of the newspaper being crushed in her hands made Clorox flinch.

An unfamiliar man sat in a chair near Brenda's. He had been typing on a laptop but stopped when Tia appeared.

"You," Tia said, as she nodded at the man. "Get the doctor now. We have an emergency! Brenda, come with me!"

Tia was about to open the door to her room when Dr. Aufseridish walked out of a room a few doors down. "What on earth is happening? Tia, where did you come from?" she asked.

"Doesn't matter. My cat got burned by those strange *matches* and needs help. Give her whatever medicine you gave me," Tia said as she rushed into her room and put Clorox on the counter. The window she had snuck through hours before was still open.

"We need to get these things off her flesh now, but gently," Brenda said as she reached for sterilized tweezers. "Or we will rip her skin clean off."

"Here, this will help," Dr. Aufseridish said as she located a vein in Clorox's back leg and injected a liquid. "It will numb the pain."

"I'll do it." Tia grabbed the tweezers from Brenda, overcome with distrust toward them and angry she had to turn to these lying bitches for help.

Dr. Aufseridish set up a bag of saline solution and a drip and attached it to Clorox. "Here, after you remove them place them in this metal bowl. Do not touch them. We don't know how long they remain active. And then put this ointment on—very generously—wherever they were."

Tia nodded and gently started to pick the little white pieces off of her cat. She did not ask what they were or any other questions at all. She knew these women were liars and had been gaslighting her about how long she'd been there. She needed their medical advice and help to save Clorox and that was all. Once her cat was strong enough, they'd leave and never come back.

"Did you jump out the window, Tia? Why on earth would you do that? We've done nothing but care for you and you snuck out in the middle of the night? Why?" Dr. Aufseridish asked.

Tia shot her an 'eat shit' look and continued working on the cat.

The guy from the hall came in and Brenda sent him to get food for Tia and something for the cat to eat. She called him Wai.

The other person that picked me up from the sidewalk, Tia thought, without looking at him.

"See how we are looking after you? Tia—*and* your cat! And you jumped out a window in the middle of the night to leave? That is so very, very dangerous. You have no idea what roams this property and these hills. No idea!" Dr. Aufseridish's voice rose.

"What roams this property and hills?" Tia asked, pausing in her endeavor to look at the doctor.

"Oh, never mind! You need to talk to Naf about that. This is his Center," Dr. Aufseridish snapped and then left the room.

Several hours later, Tia lay in bed, gently spooning Clorox. The cat's skin was pink and bloody and covered with a gray jelly-like ointment. Every half hour, Tia would check to be sure Clorox was still breathing and not in distress, and reapply the ointment.

By early evening, Clorox stirred. Tia gave her the fish Wai had brought for her and laughed—and cried—when she scarfed it down.

"Hey, slow down or you'll just puke it up," Tia said, giving her more.

After Clorox finished the fish and drank some water, she gingerly curled up at the bottom of the bed and fell asleep. Tia felt confident she would survive. The burns and sores were already shrinking in size.

Brenda and the doctor sure seemed familiar with those little pieces of flaming hot plastic. They knew exactly how to safely remove them and what medicine to use.

What is in that ointment?

Tia rummaged through drawers, looking for a box or something with a name and ingredient list. She only found the metal container full of the strange white debris she'd removed from Clorox's flesh. They sure as hell weren't matches and those two knew it! The assault was not a meth head looking for cash for a fix.

I want some goddamn truthful answers! And why do they say strange things, like that 'I belong here?' What the fuck is going on?

There were noises in the hall. Tia figured she had been locked in again. She knew no one out there would answer her questions honestly. *Ask Naf. Talk to Naf,* Dr. Aufseridish kept saying.

"You look so much better—stronger," Tia told Clorox, petting the few places that still had fur. "You rest here; I'll be back soon."

Tia grabbed the metal container of bizarre plastic bits and shoved it in her backpack. She crossed the small room and quietly opened the window. She put on her sunglasses and, like the night before, jumped out without looking down.

Ten

Tia limped along the building, staying close to the walls. She made her way to the main building and walked inside. It was silent and empty. She had no idea where "Naf," as people called him, would be. Approaching the elevator bank, she figured she might as well start at the roof garden.

Where is everyone? There are supposed to be like fifty people at this Center. I never see anyone walking around or working. Maybe that is a lie as well.

The elevator arrived and a large, dark-haired man with suntanned skin stepped out.

Tia jumped back.

A memory of this man flashed across her mind. The memory was a jumbled mess but it made Tia's heart race with fear.

"Are you supposed to be here?" he asked, his eyebrows shooting up above his glasses in surprise.

Tia took a deep, calming breath to regain her composure. She strongly felt that this man was a violent asshole but she did not know why.

"I'm looking for Naf. Have you seen him?" Tia asked.

The man cocked his head slightly. "He's at the garden party. Like everyone else. Behind the pool. But you're supposed to be in your room, recovering."

How does he know who I am?

"Oh, cool, fun. Yes, I don't look or feel party-ready. See you later," Tia said awkwardly walking quickly back to the lobby, fighting the desire to run. That man scared her.

Tia stumbled around looking for the pool. Nafasi had told her it was behind the main building, but she had not seen it.

She came across the entrance of what looked like a maze, with very tall hedges and trees blocking her view. She had a vague recollection of Nafasi talking about this garden, but try as she might, she could not remember the details. It was close to six o'clock and still very hot. Due to climate change, Pennsylvania in July was sweltering, even high up in the hills. The world had done an incredible job since the shooting to stop gas emissions, but five years was not enough time to counter seventy years of horrific pollution. Scientists said Earth may have dodged the worst-case scenarios, but for now, global warming and extreme weather were still happening.

Tia wiped the sweat off her brow as she snuck down the paved trails between the hedges and trees. There were flowers and benches in little nooks off the main paths. She passed a few colorful hammocks hanging between tall pine trees and twisted oaks. Tia inhaled deeply, enjoying the organic smells of soil, grass, trees, flowers, and farther away, goats, sheep, and other animals.

This place is so beautiful and restful. And it does seem like there are very few people here. If I had not been attacked, lied to, locked in a room, and my cat nearly killed, this could be a cool place to hang out for a while.

Rap music played in the distance. She cautiously followed the sound and recognized the beat as belonging to a very old DMX song she liked. Tia walked around a bend and jumped back; the pool was in sight and the music was much louder.

She was very close to the party.

The pool was huge and rectangular, with lounge chairs, tables, and umbrellas sprinkled around it. There was a bar at one end but no one was there. Bright-colored towels were folded and placed around the pool just so, making it appear very inviting. Tia felt an overwhelming desire to jump in the refreshing-looking pool with the bottom painted a cool indigo blue.

Tia heard glasses clink and a loud burst of laughter over the music. At the end of the pool, stone steps led up to the party. She walked over to the steps and started up them. She was crouched so low she was almost crawling up the shallow steps. At the top step, she ducked down, hoping she could see the party before the attendees could see her. However, she could not remember the last time she had taken a proper shower and had slept under a tree the night before. They might smell her before they heard or saw her.

There was a narrow grass landing, a couple of steps leading down, and another ten leading up. The path and stairs seemed to flow with the natural contour of the rolling hills. On the next flat landing was the party. Tia saw a DJ on the side on an elevated platform, or perhaps another naturally elevated flat. There was a wooden trellis on both sides, covered with vines and flowers. White columns seemed to frame the sky where the sunset would soon be. People were dancing. It was a strange angle, so she moved closer.

She moved up the steps leading to the party. Near the top step, she crouched down and stayed in the shadow of a column. She was prepared to run down the steps and back to the pool if needed. People moved about, dancing near the DJ, while some were standing around talking. She did a quick count and guessed there were around thirty in the crowd, but not Nafasi. Everyone seemed to have drinks in their hands. The floor was white, with white high-top tables and chairs sprinkled about. Several people leaned against the tables. The green of the grassy hills and the white of the party furniture against the brilliant blue sky were breathtaking. The orange sun looked like the star of the party, with clouds, sky, and everything else set up like a frame around a gorgeous painting.

Tia was transfixed by the vibrancy of the scene.

This is the perfect place to hold a party. And it will grow even more stunning as it gets closer to sunset. It would be awesome to be at a beautiful party like this, just having fun rather than confronting someone who's concealing brutal violence.

A noise from behind her caught her attention and she whipped around to find the big man that she'd talked to in the main building enter the pool area and head directly toward the steps Tia was kneeling on.

When he looked up and saw Tia hiding behind the column, his eyebrows shot up above his sunglasses and his body straightened. He seemed startled, even though he had told her exactly where to go.

He pulled a white cloth from his pocket, and it triggered a memory.

Had this man come at me with a cloth before? Did he drug me?

Tia could not clearly remember enough to accuse him.

This is what it must feel like to live and work around your rapist after being assaulted. To add insult to injury, survivors were often called 'liars' by their attackers, families, coworkers, and social workers. Even after the 'Me Too' movement, those were such horrible times for survivors. Of course, that was before the shooting and The Pledge. It's not supposed to happen anymore! I'm not letting this asshole get within ten feet of me!

Tia's heart raced as he approached her, not only because he might try to assault her, but because she feared he might call security and make her leave before she could speak to Nafasi. She had not been invited to this party and did not look like the other attendees and this man had caught her spying and knew she was not a guest.

Fuck it. It's now or never.

Tia jumped up, walked the final steps to the landing, and entered the party. She needed to find Nafasi now.

Eleven

People moved away from Tia.

Not in fear, she noticed, but something that looked like disgust.

They were all dressed casually, and yet they seemed more formal than she did. They were put together, like they had just walked out of one of those old fashion magazines that were popular before the shooting. Or perhaps the New York MET gala before The Pledge, and before environmental impacts were taken into consideration.

As Tia scanned the party, she noted that everyone appeared dynamic, radiant, and colorful. The ages seemed to range from teens to silver-haired boomers. Their features and clothes seemed almost exaggerated and far too glamorous for these Pennsylvania hills.

If Clorox looked like a calico dipped in bleach, then these people looked like figures straight off an artist's oil painting palette. One gorgeous woman was wearing a blue bathing suit in a shade so vibrant it almost hurt Tia's eyes. She paired her bathing suit with clunky white jewelry and high white heels. The DJ had blond, almost yellow, hair down her back, pale white skin, bright pink lipstick, and huge sunglasses.

She was wearing a white tank and white shorts, which again, should be casual but looked extremely stylish.

Most of the partygoers were wearing sunglasses.

What are these people? And what must they think of me? Unbathed, dirty, and wearing tan hiking pants, a ratty Outer Banks t-shirt I took from someone's dryer in Deep Creek, and clunky Keen's.

No wonder they are moving away from me.

"Hi, Tia! Welcome to our sunset shindig! Would you like a drink?" Nafasi asked, as he crossed the dance floor, his arms out in a welcoming gesture.

She was relieved to see him.

Tia's eyes were drawn to a woman standing near Nafasi. Her black hair was cut into cool jagged layers that perfectly framed her doll-like face. She was wearing a tight, sleeveless orange sundress with white flowers, the same shade of orange as the sun. She also wore cool, small, 1960s-style sunglasses. To her right stood a man with brown hair, a rugged Lincoln beard, and a tight grey v-neck shirt that showed off his muscles. On her left was a black man with dread-locks down his back, wearing white shorts, matching Converse high tops, and sunglasses. Shirtless, his chest muscles flexed as he sipped his cocktail.

They were all gorgeous.

"She smells terrible. I thought she was still locked in the medical ward. She needs to go back there imme-diately," the black-haired woman said to Nafasi.

Several people laughed at her bitchy remark.

"And she will," Nafasi said with a smile. "But for now, let's be polite, kind guests. Would you like a drink, Tia?"

"Perhaps she would like a dip in the pool. That might be more helpful," the woman said snidely. "Honestly, I can't abide her smell."

"I don't want a drink," Tia said to Nafasi. "And I don't want to be insulted again." She glared at the woman. "I just want some answers and then I will leave this bizarre place forever."

Several people chuckled.

Tia realized the DJ had stopped the music. Guests who had been further away casually moved closer. Some looked annoyed by her presence, many dramatically wrinkled their noses, while others just looked curious.

Tia put her backpack on the ground and pulled out the metal container with the white plastic-like pieces that had burned her and Clorox so badly. Tia was happy for the audience. She hoped it would reduce the chance of Nafasi lying, or, at least, help them understand the hypocrisy; how could these poisonous things be just a figment of her imagination when the doctor had a ready-made cure?

They are either witnesses or complicit in whatever is happening here.

"What are these? Why did you and the doctor say I was burned with matches when I clearly was not? Why was I locked in my room? Am I a prisoner here? And for real, how many days have I been here? If you say 48 hours, I'm going to scream."

All eyes turned toward Nafasi.

"Also, who attacked me?" Tia demanded. "What the fuck is going on here?"

"Go back to your room. This is an exclusive party. Naf will explain everything tomorrow. Or, better yet, leave Hill View Hotel Center, no one cares," the black-haired woman in the orange sundress said with a dramatic shrug.

"Fuck off, bitch. I'm talking to Nafasi," Tia said.

Nafasi laughed, genuine amusement making his face even more handsome.

"Tia, look around! Have a drink. Celebrate that you are here! Look at that beauty," he said, turning to the sky and spreading his arms wide. "We can talk about everything else tomorrow. Tonight, just enjoy yourself."

The elegant partygoers resumed their conversations. The music started back up, this time an old classic Beastie Boys song, but with the volume more subdued than the DMX song. Tia looked at the DJ and could tell she was staring back at her, even though they both had on sunglasses.

"I would rather hear the truth right now. My cat almost died. What attacked us and why?" Tia demanded.

Movement caught Tia's attention. Across the dance floor, past the high cocktail tables and up on a little grassy knoll, a man paced. He appeared as a dark silhouette, framed by the sky and sun. As Tia watched him, he stopped and stared at her and then started to slowly approach her and Nafasi. He was wearing an outfit that perfectly fit his skinny, muscular body.

Does everyone here do CrossFit? Are all their clothes tailored?

Even the partygoers noticed him, turning their heads to follow his progress across the dancefloor.

Tia gasped as he walked close enough for her to see his features. His skin was alabaster white. His eyes were a bland shade of brown, the same as his hair. As much as the other guests were vibrant with color, he was devoid of it. He was still handsome in a strange and undeniably stylish way.

The strange man suddenly and dramatically laid down on his side on an empty chaise lounge. Leaning on his elbow and resting his head on his hand, he smiled at her.

Tia could not pull her eyes away.

He tossed back his head and laughed.

Tia's blood ran cold. His mouth seemed black. It may have been the angle, but she could not see teeth, just a black gaping hole. It triggered a flashback to the assailant on her back. When she attempted to head bump him, he had shifted his weight and she caught a glimpse of him. She thought she saw a bright white form and a black gaping hole.

Is this the man that assaulted me? Who shoved me into the concrete, gave me a concussion, and tried to burn me alive? Here, at this fucking sunset shindig?

"Okay well, I suppose Ash is right," Nafasi said, changing his tune. "You probably should head back to your room and get some rest. You seem very anxious and it's not necessary. Parties are supposed to be fun. Go with Doc and Brenda and I will see you tomorrow. Is that okay? We can discuss everything tomorrow. I think that will be for the best, okay?" Nafasi smiled, nodding his head at her and the other guests.

It was only then that Tia noticed that Dr. Aufseridish and Brenda had walked up the steps and were standing close by.

Brenda took the metal container from Tia's hand and picked up her backpack. She put the container inside and offered the bag to Tia.

Dr. Aufseridish gently took Tia's arm. Seeing them here, surrounded by these shiny, pretty people, Tia realized they were both rather bland. The doctor was attractive but did not have the exaggerated perfection of the guests. Tia remembered she was from the Middle East. She also seemed to be dressed like a mortal, rather than like these movie stars. *Where are these fashionistas from?*

"Come with us. You can shower and eat and, when you feel better, can rejoin the party. You're a guest here," Dr. Aufseridish said soothingly as she guided Tia back down the stairs and toward the pool.

Okay, fine. I'm just happy to get away from that freak.

In the few minutes that she had been at the party, the space around the pool had filled up with people, many as vibrant and elegantly dressed as those on the upper landing. The DJ had resumed her set at a higher volume. The pool bar now had a bartender, and people sat on barstools, talking and drinking. One side of the pool had the high hedges that Tia had walked along to find the party. The other side of the pool had a gray stone wall at least six feet high. Tia had not noticed it before; she had been more intrigued by the pool, and probably would not have noticed it now, except that there were three men, around her age, sitting on it. They were holding beers and joking around with one another. As she walked by, they all stared at her.

Tia tried to ignore everyone staring at her and she picked up the pace, but something about one of the young men on the wall caught her attention. She locked eyes with the guy who crashed her Deep Creek sanctuary and recommended she come to this place.

Twelve

Tia looked away hurriedly and leaned more into the doctor.

What the fuck? Just act weak and helpless in front of these freaks, get back to the room, grab Clorox, and get the fuck out of here. This was some kind of a set-up or a trap. Maybe they lure hermits like me into their bizarre cult and burn them alive or feed us to that freak!

As soon as Tia was in the hedge maze and out of eyeshot of the partygoers, she shrugged off Dr. Aufseridish and walked ahead of her escorts. She was infuriated, confused, and scared. Every once in a while, Brenda or the doctor would yell directions if Tia veered off in the wrong direction.

Tia slammed through the main door of the building but, this time, avoided the elevator. She roamed around until she found a stairwell and ran up the three flights, skipping every other step. When she got to the door of the room where she had been staying, she opened the door quietly, not wanting to scare Clorox.

What the fuck!

Clorox was not on the bed. The sheets had been removed and it was just a bare mattress. The room was so clean it seemed like no one had recently stayed there.

"Tia, we moved your cat into another room. We needed to clean up and you need a proper room. This was once a hotel. It has great rooms and there is no reason for you to stay in the medical area," Brenda explained as she entered the room. "Come with me and I will show you to your new room."

Tia followed Brenda, eager to see Clorox. Brenda led Tia back to the stairs, up two floors, and down a long hallway.

"This is a lovely room," Brenda said as she opened the door. "It has a full bathroom, stocked with all the things you should need. We put some clean clothes in the drawers. There's food and drinks in the minifridge for both you and your cat, and wait until you see the view."

Tia locked eyes with Clorox as she entered the room. They had put down towels and blankets for the cat to lay on rather than the pretty bedspread, but of course, the cat avoided those. She was bathing herself on the small, exposed area of the bedspread between the pillows.

Clorox was very much improved. Her eyes looked clear, her energy was back enough to be bathing, and she moved as though she was offended to be there. However, her skin still looked angry, pink, and greasy.

"Okay then, that sounds like everything. Thanks, Brenda," Tia said as she pushed Brenda out of the room and slammed the door.

"Of course, no lock," Tia mumbled as she examined the knob. "At least not on this side. Oh, and yes

Clorox, let's look at the view." Tia stomped to the window. The sun had moved further down and the sky was full of blue, pink, and purple shades. Tia could not take her eyes off of it for a full thirty seconds. It was dazzling. "Of course, the view is not the point. I don't think I can jump from a fifth-floor window without doing some damage, as they well know."

When she could pull her eyes away, she moved to the bed and lay down next to Clorox.

"How are you feeling? You look better. Not sure it's a good idea to lick off all that medicine," Tia said when she realized what the cat was doing. "Oh well, I guess it's not killing you. I think I'd better clean up too. Some fucking bitch told me I smell and people laughed. Can you believe that? They tried to kill me— us. They locked me up, lied to me, *then* insulted me. And they are just plain strange."

Tia quickly showered, ate, and put on clean clothes.

"As soon as you feel strong enough, we are out of here," Tia told Clorox as she hand-fed her some white flaky fish. Clorox did appear significantly better. She had gone from nearly dead to nearly recovered in just a day. Tia decided she would take some of the ointment with her when they left.

"But not at night. I'm way more afraid of the freak at the party than any tiger or made-up meth-head mugger. One way or another, we leave at first light," Tia told Clorox. The cat started to purr.

Thirteen

Tia woke up just before dawn from a restless night. Clorox was sitting next to the door with an annoyed look on her face.

"I know, I want out of here too," she whispered to the cat.

Tia quickly freshened up and made sure she had the metal container with the plastic bits inside, what was left of the magic ointment, and her sunglasses. She also took some of the clothes Brenda had left for her.

She was very surprised when the door opened and even more surprised to see an empty hall. She quietly rushed to the stairwell and descended to the lobby level. Clorox stayed close. The main door was unlocked as well. When she was out in the early morning air, she felt an enormous wave of relief.

As they quickly walked down the hill, they stayed as far off the road as they could, in case they had to hide amongst the trees. When the trees thinned into open fields, Tia would jog to quickly pass through the exposed areas.

In the light of day, Tia questioned what had happened and what she had seen.

Did that strange guy attack me? What was wrong with his mouth? Why did those people look so odd? Why would a bunch of fashionistas and models come way out here to the middle of nowhere? What does this Center do?

And, holy shit, that lying sack of shit thief just sat there, enjoying the party! Of course, he is not the only liar!

Exactly how long have I been there? It sure as hell has not been forty-eight hours! What the fuck is going on? At the same time, I don't want to know. Not my business. I just want out of this fucked up place and on my way. I just want to get back to the bus station and sweet talk someone into paying my fare to somewhere far away from here.

As they passed the first house they came upon, Tia was relieved it was still very early. She doubted anyone was awake yet. She thought the town seemed like it was full of late-rising people. As they walked down the hill, they began passing houses that were closer to the road.

Something caught Tia's eye and made her stop dead in her tracks.

A flash of pain and terror rushed through her body as a vivid memory of a hard push and harder landing entered her mind. What caught her attention were the bits of white plastic on the sidewalk and the road. Her heart started to race and she could hear the blood rushing through her ears.

Before I put the pieces in my backpack, they were picked out of Clorox's burnt flesh. What the fuck is it?

Tia squatted down to count them. There were more than twenty on the sidewalk where Tia assumed she landed and a few sprinkled in the road. There was also a little trail leading off the sidewalk and into an empty wooded lot.

I bet this is where he doused me with those things, and the ones in the road fell off when Brenda and Wai put me in their vehicle. I bet the rest fell off Clorox when she ran. Or maybe they fell off my assailant? We were careful to use tweezers and not touch them but how come Brenda and Wai did not get burned when they picked me up? And no way in hell this shit looks like matches. Even though it's been a few days, I'm scared to touch them. How many days has it been? Seriously, how many fucking days has it been?

A woman with a large dog was suddenly only two feet away. Startled, Tia fell over onto her butt. "What the fuck!"

"I'm sorry to startle you! I figured you heard us coming," the woman said, sounding a little defensive.

Tia quickly got up and jumped around, in case any of those little white pieces had stuck on her.

"Oh, you're the woman who was attacked! Well, you look a lot better than when I saw you last week!" the woman said in a strong Pennsylvania accent.

"You found me?" Tia asked.

"Yes, we did. Johnny and I walk up this way all the time. Imagine my shock to find a woman lying right there, bleeding, unconscious, smelling as though she was on fire. I was afraid you were going to die! I flipped you over because I thought maybe you landed on a joint or something when you fell, but then I realized you were burned by some kind of creepy matches. We don't have a hospital or emergency services here so I called up to the Hill View Hotel and asked them for help. I mean, from the look of you, you were coming or going from there.”

“What do you mean? ‘From the look of me?’ Assaulted and on fire?” Tia asked.

The woman looked Tia up and down. “You know, you look really good. Healed. I’m just happy it worked out. I need to get going. Finish our walk before the kids get up,” the woman said and started to walk away.

“Wait, please. I’m sorry. Let me start over. I’m Tia. You’re right, I was heading to the hotel. And I’m very grateful that you found me and reported it. You saved my life. I can’t thank you enough,” Tia said.

A huge smile spread across the woman’s face. She stuck out her hand. “I’m Caitlin. Nice to meet you, Tia. And anytime! Helping you was the most exciting thing to happen around here in forever.”

“Can I walk with you and Johnny?” Tia asked.

“Sure. We usually go halfway up the hill to get exercise. But since I assume you just came down, maybe we should walk into town?” Caitlin suggested.

“That would be fine,” Tia said, hiding her relief. She knew going into town was high risk and she should shove off in case any of those freaks came after her, but she had so many questions and Caitlin seemed to have answers.

“That night is fuzzy for me. Do you mind if I ask you questions about it?” Tia asked.

“No, of course not. But it’s kind of fuzzy for me as well. I was walking up the hill and it was dark, just a sliver of a moon. If we had not been walking on this side of the street on the sidewalk, I may not have seen you. If Johnny wasn’t a few steps ahead and smelled you, I may have tripped over you. I was watching a video on my phone," Caitlin explained.

Tia nodded, encouraging her to continue.

"I was like, 'What the hell!' Like I said, I could smell burning hair and skin. I bent down and rolled you over. Your eyes were a little open, but you were not there. I shook you and checked your neck for a pulse, which you had obviously, or we would not be having this conversation right now," Caitlin said.

"Who answered the phone at the hotel?" Tia asked.

"I don't know. I just dialed the main line. Maybe it was Mr. Nafasi? They probably introduced themselves but I don't recall. I just explained that a woman was lying on the sidewalk just past where the single-family houses started on the road up the hill and she was in very bad shape, bleeding, unconscious and she looked to me like one of their guests. They said they would inform their doctor and send someone down immediately. Which they did. Two people arrived here within like fifteen minutes. While I was waiting, I called my wife and told her what was up and she stayed on the line with me until they arrived. She wanted to come out—she was frantic—but I told her to stay with the kids. That's why I left as soon as they arrived," Caitlin continued. "Seriously, I high-tailed it the minute their vehicle arrived."

Tia pictured the assault and the timeline, remembering the pain and fear.

"You and your wife were afraid that whoever jumped me was still around." It dawned on her how frightening it must have been for Caitlin.

"Yes. Johnny is a large dog but, as you can see, is as gentle as they come. I hoped he looked intimidating enough, in case whoever did that to you came back. Or was still around, watching us," Caitlin added.

"Did you see anyone?" Tia asked.

"Not a soul. It was quiet. Just insects and normal night creatures. I sat by you and kept saying you were going to be okay, to soothe you, me, and my wife," Caitlin said with a laugh. "Anyway, Mr. Nafasi texted me the next day and said you were okay and healing fast. It's personal and I don't judge anyone, ever, I mean we all deal with the world the way we do, okay? But he wrote that the hotel had not been expecting you and he suspected you were on drugs, and it may have been a drug deal gone bad. He thought the hotel, I mean the Center, could help you. Like I said, you look really good now, so all is well," Caitlin said.

Interesting story. The only drugs I enjoy occasionally are tobacco and weed and they are legal. I have not smoked pot in months. No way the doctor thought I was on drugs.

"Nafasi is his first name. They all call him Naf. I can't remember his last name." Tia explained absentmindedly as she thought through the numerous drug accusations.

"Oh, okay, good to know," Caitlin replied.

"Are there a lot of drug dealers here?" Tia asked. "Are violent assaults common?"

Caitlin sighed. "There used to be. We were a meth capital for a while and had all the violence that comes with that. Like many Pennsylvanian towns, we lost our main employer—this town made car upholstery for decades. Then the great economic depression of

2008 and 2009 hit. After the drug issues and over-doses, the pandemic, and the mass shooting, it's shocking anyone is still here. Half of these houses and businesses are vacant. We lost almost half the adults in this town on July 14 and a lot of kids too. It was a big hunting town. Many of those that survived left. We have had some people move back. We've had orphans move in with relatives—lots of orphans. My wife and I are schoolteachers, so we are keenly aware of when kids move here. Anyway, it's still a big mess. But no, no violence for a long time."

"Why do you stay?" Tia asked.

"This is home. My wife was born here. Me, in a town not far from here. And people are trying. We have community gardens, and we share and help each other a lot more than before the shooting. It's a community in its own way. The government helps keep the school open. All the kids go to one school now. Not enough kids or teachers for more. Some people lost so much they just don't get out of bed. They're still in deep mourning and dealing with PTSD from the shock of it all. Between the injuries and the survivor's guilt, maybe they will never get over the shooting. But in some ways, things are getting better. We do look after each other. We walk gently on the planet. Most of us try to adhere to The Pledge. And, if you can see past the abandoned buildings and peeling paint, it is pretty. The woods, rivers, and hills are gorgeous, and wildlife is thriving again. We have beavers back in the cricks. It's like nature is encouraging us to keep going. We just need time." Caitlin paused in front of a house and unleashed Johnny. He ran to the screen door and opened it with his nose, disappearing into the house.

"And that was the long way of saying I'm not judging your drug use and I'm happy you are better. I think, in my mind, you were worse than you were. I told folks you had a huge gash on your forehead and blood all over your face, your hands and knees were bleeding, and you were burning all over, but I must have remembered it worse than it was. Maybe the adrenaline and fear made it seem more serious. If you had all those other injuries, no way you would look this good so soon. I barely even see a bruise on you," Caitlin said, smiling.

Okay, that's my cue to go. It always amazes people how fast I heal. Even without the doctor's miracle ointment, I would have healed fast.

"What can I say? I'm young and healthy. Thanks again for saving me and explaining this and well … everything." Tia bowed her head slightly and moved her hands into a namaste position.

"I mean, I guess it has been a week, right? It's the 12th and I found you on the 4th. The Fourth of July is usually quiet around here since people don't do fireworks anymore. Finding you was the holiday excitement," Caitlin said.

July 12th? I have been at the Center for seven fucking days? I knew 48 hours was bullshit! Clorox could have died! Why all the lies?

"But still, miraculous healing. Now that I think about it, you were lucky the Center was occupied since Monday is the anniversary of the shooting. For the past two years, they have emptied out the Center around the anniversary. I don't know why; we just see a lot of SUVs and cars go by as they head out of town in late June, and then they return at some point after the anniversary. We don't communicate much with the Center," Caitlin said, looking back up the hill.

"You personally or the locals in general?" Tia asked.

"Everyone. There are some issues with the Center not hiring more locals, especially since it was a thriving hotel at one point. And some people think it's a cult." Caitlin shrugged. "But I don't judge. Live and let live, I mean if they are helping people like you, that's great."

People like me? Drug addicts?

"Tia, I did see your eyes last week and they looked pretty intense. I think you should allow people to help you. I mean, it was partly your eyes that made me think you were heading to the Center," Caitlin added.

"Caitlin, breakfast is ready," a woman impatiently called from the other side of the dark screen door.

Johnny pushed out through the door and a small boy followed.

"I'm coming in a minute, Finn," Caitlin said, smiling at the child. "Go back inside."

"Mom says the internet is down or something. The computers are going crazy again. She needs your help," Finn replied.

"I guess it's not just breakfast they want me for. We've had so many computer problems lately. All our electronics are on the blink. Even our solar panels have been malfunctioning. It's annoying and strange. Has the Center been having problems?" Caitlin asked.

"None that I noticed. Thanks again, Caitlin," Tia said, happy for the distraction before Caitlin could ask about her eyes. "I should get going. I hope your stuff starts working soon." Tia walked down the sidewalk and into town, happy she was wearing sunglasses.

Fourteen

Tia spotted the bus station up ahead and picked up her pace. She hoped she could get on for free since she did not have any money. The government almost completely subsidized any activities that reduced carbon emissions so buses were practically free. She glanced behind her to make sure Clorox was following along.

"You need to get in this backpack to get on the bus. I should dump the clothes because you still look sticky, though maybe the clothes will make it softer for you," Tia said to Clorox as they drew nearer to the bus station. Tia cringed at how pink and vulnerable the little cat looked with so much fur missing on her back. "How did you survive for so many days without the medicine? They put that goo on me the first night. It's so strange how tough you are. How did you get burned? When that monster jumped me, you should've run away."

The man at the party flashed through Tia's mind, causing her heart to quicken and her feet to jog. "Come on. No more fucking around, we need to get out of this town," Tia called over her shoulder to the cat.

It was still early, and Tia had only seen a few cars since she left Caitlin's house, but just as she was about to cross the last street between her and the bus station, a shiny electric Cadillac SUV idled in front of her. The passenger side window came down.

"Hey, Tia. How's it going?" Nafasi asked from behind the steering wheel. He raised his voice somewhat to be heard across the passenger seat.

Fuck, I did not want an awkward conversation with this dude. At least he's alone.

"Hi, Nafasi. I'm good, thanks. I need to be going. Thanks again for the help and hospitality at the Center, but I need to be getting back home," Tia said, as fake friendly as she could muster.

You lied to me. You might be harboring a psychopath. And now you're stalking me. Fuck off.

"We need to talk. Please come back up to the Center so we can have a real conversation," Nafasi said, looking worried. He indicated she should open the passenger door and climb in.

"No thanks, I need to scoot. But, you know, thanks again," Tia said, allowing anger to crawl into her words.

Nafasi casually put the car in park, turned off the engine, stepped out, and walked around the bumper with a small smile on his face.

Damn, he is good-looking, Tia thought as he approached her. He was wearing sunglasses, a tight navy crew-cut t-shirt, light blue cut-off denim shorts that went almost to his knees, and running shoes. There was nothing special about his clothes, yet they seemed so stylish and perfectly form-fitting. In the morning light, his hair seemed more orange than auburn and he reminded Tia of Harry, the Regent of England.

"Tia, we got off to a bad start. If you had not been assaulted, our introduction would have been so much better. We would have had the difficult conversation already. You would realize you are in a safe space here. You would probably love the Center already. Come on, those hills? That view? The sunsets and gardens? It's paradise! And we both know you do not have a home to rush off to or any place to be," he said, dramatically taking off his Ray-Ban sunglasses.

His eyes were so light blue they looked more like an animal's eyes. His features did not match his tanned skin at all. *He must spend a lot of time at his pool,* Tia thought.

A blue Amazon van pulled up behind Nafasi's Cadillac and Nafasi took a couple of steps toward it and waved good-naturedly, indicating it should go around. Tia and Nafasi watched it pass and turn the corner. There was a United States Postal Service emblem on the back.

"Don't know why they still bother with both emblems. Amazon owns the Postal Service; people should just accept it. Amazon does a better job anyway. How would we have survived the pandemic and every-thing without the Amazon army, am I right? Even way out here, you can get what you need within a few days," he commented.

"I'm happy we still have the Postal Service. It's his-toric and it has brought a strong union to Amazon," Tia countered. She had a deep hatred of rich people and monopolies owned by billionaires. Their greed and selfishness caused global warming, the biodiversity extinction crisis, and probably the collision that brought Rex's wrath to Earth.

"Yes, but due to The Pledge, everything is basically unionized now. Though I think it's a stretch to say making employees work a full day might bring Rex back," Nafasi continued. "But that doesn't matter, right? I'm here to convince you, and your cat, to come up to the Center—to relax and study and learn and enjoy yourself for a few weeks. Hang out by the pool, take some hikes, and, assuming we get the solar panels working, enjoy the library and game room in the AC. It's getting hot already. Let's go up the hill. Even without power, it's cooler up there," Nafasi said, waving his arm toward his Cadillac.

"What is going on with the panels?" Tia was curious since Caitlin had mentioned problems as well.

"Oh, shit is happening. The Internet is down. Electricity is spotty. Things are crazy. You might not even be able to get a bus today," Nafasi said with a big smile.

"Are you doing it? Causing it from the Center?" Tia asked.

"Ha, no. It's happening to us as well. It's happening all over the world. In the grand scheme of things, it's a good thing. Let's go up to the Center, get you your meal for the day, and talk about it, okay?" He still had a relaxed smile on his face.

Tia realized this crazy thing happening may have been why she was able to leave so easily this morning. Perhaps Nafasi and his staff were distracted by the power outage.

A black Tesla and another white Cadillac SUV pulled up behind Nafasi's vehicle. He did not wave them around.

"It's time to go, Tia," he said, putting his sunglasses on.

The cars had lined up on the cross street, blocking her way to the bus station. Tia took two steps into the main road leading out of town. She saw what looked like a bus far off, but moving quickly toward the town.

"I think a bus is coming now. I need to be on it. People seem to be inside the station so I'm fine," Tia said as she walked in front of Nafasi's parked vehicle to cross the street.

"That's not a bus. It's a truck. I think it's from the government and I'm pretty sure it's coming for you," Nafasi said, peering over his sunglasses at the quickly approaching truck.

This is total manipulative bullshit. Fuck this guy.

"No way. Why would the government want to talk to me?" Tia asked.

"I don't know. Have you violated The Pledge? Committed any crimes? Have strange eyes?" He opened the passenger door and indicated with his head that she needed to get in. "Come on Tia, we need to go!" Nafasi said with urgency in his voice.

"Tia," Wai called from the Cadillac. Tia had been so focused on what she still hoped was a bus that she had not heard him get out of his car. "Tia," he called again, and this time he held Clorox up for a couple of seconds before tossing her in the back seat. He calmly shut the door and got in.

"What the fuck?" Tia yelled, but Wai was already driving away.

"If you want to see your cat alive, you'd better get in," Nafasi said in a strange voice.

Tia just stared at him.

"Ever see an old James Cagney gangster movie? Nafasi asked, smiling.

Tia did not respond.

"No? Okay. But seriously, get in," he said, no longer smiling.

"You people suck," Tia snapped, but did as she was told.

The tires squealed as Nafasi drove quickly through town.

Fifteen

afasi raced back to the Center.

Tia seethed in silence. She had not seen Wai's car since he drove away with Clorox.

Now they have abducted my cat and are holding her hostage. These people really want us in their cult.

"I'm sure she will be in your room, curled up and purring on your comfortable bed when you get back. Brenda will bring her fresh fish and she will be treated with all the respect due to a good sidekick," Nafasi said in a soothing voice. "We are here to help you, Tia. We are the good guys."

Tia fumed, looking out the window. "I thought you said everyone was vegan. Why do you have fish?" Tia asked accusatorily, catching him in another lie.

"*Most* everyone. And as you know, we have some animals, including tigers, around," Nafasi answered.

"And I'm not in trouble with the police or anyone. I'm not on drugs or a dealer. I just don't like talking to them," Tia snapped.

"Me neither," Nafasi replied.

After they parked, Tia got out of the car, slammed the door, and stomped behind the main building to the one with the medical ward where she had been staying. She shoved the doors open so hard that they hit the walls, chipping the paint

"Hey, be careful," the large man that she believed may have drugged her shouted from behind a desk in the lobby.

"Go fuck yourself," Tia responded.

That guy gives me the creeps, Tia thought, as a memory of him coming at her crossed her mind.

She ran up the stairs and charged into her room, hoping what Nafasi said was true.

There was Clorox, sitting on the windowsill, looking out at the view. The cat glanced at Tia and then looked back out the window.

Great. My cat is taken in by it too.

"I'm so happy you are okay! How did Wai get you? You're usually so stealthy. Half the time, I can't even find you. Everything here is so strange," Tia said as she opened the fridge and pulled out some fish. "Just like he said."

"Here, eat, rest and I will be back soon. What is so interesting out there anyway?" Tia tossed her sunglasses on the bed and joined Clorox at the window. The sun was up, the sky was blue, and puffy clouds were floating about. The different shades of green popped against the sky, like a painting. She saw several people talking in the splendid green terraced garden. Off in the distance, a few sheep and goats grazed. Tia wondered where the tigers were. The window was closed, and the people were too far away to hear the conversation, but she made out a loud peal of laughter.

"They do look happy, don't they?" Tia asked Clorox. "What is this place? Who are these people?"

Guess I need to go and find out.

Tia made sure Clorox had fresh water and located a litterbox someone had provided.

"I will be back to get you soon and we will leave this place for good," Tia said as she headed out the door, reminding herself not to be seduced by all the beauty.

Running down the stairs and through the lobby, tossing another "go fuck yourself" over her shoulder at the big guy still sitting at the desk, she went back to the main building where Nafasi had dropped her off. She skirted around the building, heading toward the wraparound porch that led into the gorgeous lobby. As the porch came into view, Tia stopped short and rushed back behind the corner. Several people in business suits and a few in all-black getups that resembled SWAT uniforms were speaking to Nafasi and Wai.

Who dresses to intimidate anymore?

Tia peeked around the corner. She could not hear the conversation, because she was too far away. Plus, several distracting ladybugs were munching on aphids in the bush beside her. Nafasi seemed relaxed, even patting one of the well-dressed men on the back. Though they were under the porch roof and not in the morning sunshine, Wai and Nafasi had on sunglasses.

She watched Nafasi lead them back toward the parking area.

Oh, fuck this, Tia thought as she slowly headed toward the main lobby doors, watching the group walk toward the cars. One of the people in all black turned and looked straight at Tia. Her heart raced. The person was wearing a helmet and a full faceguard.

They stared at Tia for a few seconds, before turning around and catching up with the group just as they turned the bend to the parking lot.

Shit, I don't have sunglasses! Oh well, that cop or whatever is too far to notice my eyes.

As she entered the lobby, she found Dr. Aufseridish walking toward her, as though intending to leave through the doors Tia had just passed through.

"Hi Tia, how are you feeling?" she asked in a friendly voice.

"Fine. Who were those people?"

"What people? I didn't see any people. Maybe more guests? That would be nice with all the parties and activities planned this weekend," Dr. Aufseridish replied.

"Parties? I heard you all clear out around the 14th. Why not this year?" Tia asked.

"This year is different—special. You should ask Nafasi to explain," she said.

"Why can't you tell me?" Tia asked, exasperated. "I don't trust a word out of that liar's mouth."

"Tia! I don't know if he lied or what he lied about. I don't know what you've discussed. But it seems to me you have not had a real, meaningful conversation yet, or you would not be this confused and hostile. Honestly, Tia, just talk with him. He is my boss and this is his Center so you need to talk to him," Dr. Aufseridish said, sounding annoyed.

Wai pushed through the lobby doors. "Naf wants to talk to both of you at the pool. He wants you to join him for breakfast," Wai said. He was relaxed, as though he had not just been surrounded by the SWAT team that had rattled Nafasi downtown.

Tia sighed loudly.

Had he just been acting scared to bring her back here?

"Okay, sure, cat abductor. Let's go hear what the head liar has to say," Tia snapped. "And you'd better never fucking touch my cat again. Ever."

Sixteen

Tia sat at a rectangular table near the pool. There was some old-school heavy metal playing quietly in the background. The table was covered with food. Nafasi sat at one end, and Dr. Aufseridish at the other, with Tia in the middle.

"Like I said yesterday, most of our food is produced here, in the gardens or the greenhouse. Some comes from exchanges with local farmers. Anyway, eat, please. We all need one good meal a day. I'm ravenous after all the excitement this morning. Tia, perhaps you feel the same?" Nafasi asked.

Tia took a piece of sprouted bread and slowly chewed, waiting to finally have the important conversation Dr. Aufseridish had been referencing since the day she arrived. The one that would supposedly answer all her questions and make her understand what this place was and why she was there.

"First, we will begin at my beginning. I was always fascinated by space. I felt confident that there was life elsewhere and was determined to communicate with these other societies. My parents happily indulged my interest. I went to Space Camp in Alabama, interned with the greatest minds at NASA, jumped from University to University while learning all I could. I was not looking for a career, I was looking for knowledge. I studied all the primitive languages and our previous attempts at intergalactic communication; Lincos, Astraglossa, Carl Sagan and the Lone Signal Transmissions, the old Pioneer and Voyager Probes, and, of course, the Arecibo and Cosmic Call messages," Nafasi explained.

Tia just nodded her head as though she understood what any of those things were.

"Have you tried our apples? It's a Gala, just picked the other day. Here, please do. It's divine," Nafasi said, handing Tia a plate of sliced apples.

Tia waved them away.

"And that all brought me to the Teen-Age Message and the Evpatoria Deep Space Center. So fascinating! I spent a lot of time in Ukraine. It's a fantastic place with amazing people. Are you familiar with the Teen-Age Message?" Nafasi asked.

"Nope, is it new dope slang?" Tia asked sarcastically.

"In layman's terms, it contained three sections: a radio signal, analog representing music, and then Arecibo binary digital info—basically "Hello, aliens" in Russian and English. But it's history now as the world was quickly moving forward. I spent a lot of time in Green Bank, West Virginia, and Socorro, New Mexico, learning about their radio telescopes. I met a lot of brilliant scientists, astrophysicists, and engineers and learned so much, but then I met the real movers and shakers in the space exploration world: the billionaires. They adopted me as one of their own since I'm very rich," Nafasi said, sounding a little annoyed. "Tia, are you following this?"

"Yes, yes, somewhat, go on," Tia replied, trying to stifle a yawn.

"We were on a quest to learn about other worlds. It was a noble quest, led by NASA and many nations. But the billionaire space boys were unabashedly about ego, money, and power. Who would be the first to outer space, then the moon, then Mars, and beyond? They were racing to try and get the first tourists up, excited about how much could they charge. How fast could they drill for minerals and metals? How much money could they make? Hell, one douchebag wore a t-shirt that said 'Colonize Mars,' and Americans just cheered him on, without giving a thought to how insulting it was to all the colonized nations on Earth, where indigenous people still suffer because of selfish, greedy people. The egotistical, power-hungry, greedy behavior of these men was not a total surprise, but the way regular people and politicians just cheered them on, never asking important questions. It was disturbing, watching history repeating. It was like they were brainwashed—or *space*washed," Nafasi continued.

"Like a cult, a cult of personalities," Tia said.

"Yes, exactly, Tia. Well, we can see where all that unregulated and selfish behavior got us: a planet surrounded by deadly garbage and a collision that resulted in hundreds of millions of lost lives," Nafasi said.

"I blame NASA and the other nations' space programs as much as the rich space bros. They started it decades ago. They could've regulated it. They could have educated Americans on the dangerous situation. One good thing that came from the mass shooting was that it called attention to the crisis in space. No one trusts those rich space assholes anymore," Tia said.

"Yes, I agree, Tia. That takes us up to the massive collision in 2019. I followed the news and helped collect the debris. It consumed me and I abandoned my research on the best languages and mechanisms for communicating with extraterrestrials for some time. But using the equipment I acquired from the collision, I created some fantastic technology and made machines that had never even been thought of before. There were materials, and metals, from the collision that were full of nitrogen! Stuff not of Earth!" Nafasi said with great enthusiasm. "With my new equipment and ideas, well, let's just say I spent a lot more time in Ukraine with the Evpatoria Planetary Radar."

Nafasi laughed to himself and clapped his hands.

Tia just nodded and continued to pick at the breakfast food. *What the hell is he talking about? Is he insane?*

"Okay, let's begin at the beginning—the part that impacts you and everyone else," Nafasi said. "I created this Center for people that were traumatized by 2020. The coronavirus pandemic shut down the world in March. Thousands of people died every day. Cable news ran twenty-four-hour death counts, hospitals were overflowing, and no one knew how it spread. We wore masks, washed everything, socially distanced, and obsessively watched the news. Then July 14th happened and many gun owners turned their weapon on themselves. More than seventy million Americans died within fifteen minutes, and hundreds of millions worldwide," Nafasi said, no longer smiling. He seemed to be watching Tia for a reaction.

Tia glanced at Dr. Aufseridish, who was nodding her head at Nafasi, encouraging him to continue. She seemed riveted. Tia looked back at Nafasi and just shrugged, reaching for some berries.

"In time, we learned, thanks to Kate Stellute and Dr. Sinclair Jones, that it was caused by a pissed-off extraterrestrial called Rex, who was angry because the collision killed his parents. The same collision where I found the technology that might change our world. Anyway, the collision was caused by human activity that created enormous amounts of pollution in space. Then we learned his colleagues did not think he had done enough to punish us. Kate said Rex was supposed to destroy the planet, but he didn't. Instead, Rex gave us a chance, but 'the others" did not agree so we—the entire world—waited for them to decide if they would destroy us all. We stared at a bizarre, unnatural cloud that read "They're here" for almost twenty-four hours. We did not know if we would die on Earth or escape to space. We didn't know if we would die there or be protected by Rex. It was truly terrifying," Nafasi said, pausing to take a long sip of tea. "Of course, this all happened in less than a year. 2020 was a total bitch. People were burying their dead, mourning enormous loss, and afraid that civilization would collapse. Amazingly, we did not all crack under the pressure and lose our minds."

Tia had heard enough. "I know all this—I was there. And we didn't go nuts because Kate and Sinclair were such badass heroes. Rex communicated with Kate and, sometimes, with Sinclair. They kept us in the loop and were completely transparent about what they knew. Kate created The Pledge to make the world better, kinder, and cleaner to convince the others we had learned our lesson. That we could change. That is why we did not crack under the pressure. Not because of the government or corporations or rich men with exotic tools. Not because of cults or Centers like this one. It was Kate and Sinclair that saved us!"

"Now who sounds a little culty?" Nafasi said, smiling. "That sounds like hero worship to me."

"Go on, Naf, tell her the good part," Dr. Aufseridish said.

"Okay, so we agree on what happened," Nafasi said. "The pandemic, the shooting, the cloud warning, all of it, created stress, loss, and sadness. When I realized that the world was going to move forward and we were going to survive, I thought, how can I help? What can I do? So, I bought the hotel and expanded the gardens, built the greenhouse, and made a yoga studio, meditation rooms, and classrooms where we can discuss our experiences and emotions and, most importantly, heal. We have Doc here to help with any medical issues that arise. She researches and creates new medicines. But most of her work with guests is drug-related problems like self-medicating."

"I don't have a drug problem. There was no drug deal gone wrong. I was violently attacked; I believe by one of your guests!" Tia, exploded, shocked that they were still trying to gaslight her with that bullshit story.

"Please, just listen, okay?" Nafasi said with a smile. "People handled the constant crises differently. Here, we help people understand that there is nothing they can do about *anything*. They can't change the past. They can't control the future, except how they respond emotionally. We help people focus on positive emotions so they can move forward and learn to enjoy life again. We are surrounded by beauty. We have everything we could ever need. We live connected and in balance with nature."

"Jesus, this is a fucking cult," Tia snapped.

"No, wait … hang-on, Tia. We are living The Pledge. Well, the best we can most of the time. And we are focusing on the positive, being healthy, and appreciating what we have. If you want to call it a cult, so be it," Nafasi explained calmly.

At that moment, a man approached the table. Tia gasped. It was the guy that she met at Deep Creek, who told her about this place and stole her phone. He'd been sitting on the wall at the party the night before.

"Sorry to interrupt, Naf, but the power is out again. The panels are getting sun, but the grid is down. We are switching to the backup solar generators but even they seem to be having problems. We might have to go to the emergency generators. It's so strange. Anyway, the internet is down, everything. They told me to let you know," the man said.

There was suddenly a strange sound far off, like an alarm of some kind. Everyone looked in the direction of a distant hill.

"I guess someone has power up there," the man from Deep Creek said to no one in particular.

"These solar flares are a nightmare and blessing. We don't have time to waste. Go ahead with whatever emergency action is necessary," Nafasi said, with a pleasant smile, giving the impression it was not a real emergency.

"Sure thing, Naf. Nice to see you again, Tia. We should catch up later," the man from Deep Creek said calmly, nodding in her direction.

"Not until the project is back on track, okay? Thanks." Nafasi waved him away. "Where was I?" he asked, as the man walked away.

"That man lied to me and stole my phone," Tia said. "You sure have a lot of scumbags in your cult. Or, I guess, I should be controlling my feelings about it, right? It's not their problem they steal, cheat, lie, and assault people. No, no, it's *my* problem because I have negative feelings about it. For instance, I'm feeling rage right now. I guess I should control my emotions, and just have positive thoughts, and if they do it again, well, I should shrug it off. Nothing anyone can do about it, right?"

Tia looked from Naf to Dr. Aufseridish indignantly.

"Hell, I tried to leave, but you kidnapped my cat, so I should accept this situation and turn my frown upside down, right? Am I understanding the teachings of your cult? I assume your emergency generators run on some carbon-based fuel, so you are contributing to global warming, which is still going to kill us all. Oh, whoops! Here I am being unhappy about something that is being done to me that I can't control. Kick me out of the fucking cult, please!" Tia snapped.

"Climate change is still a huge problem. The town has severe flooding in the spring, sometimes in the summer now too. That is why many of the homes are abandoned. Losing a third of the world's population in one year really helped, but we are still in for decades of extreme weather," Dr. Aufseridish said, finally jumping into the conversation.

"You are contributing to global warming, and housing violent criminals and liars. You'd better watch out or Rex might come back," Tia said, pushing her plate away.

Nafasi and Dr. Aufseridish laughed. Since Nafasi was taking a sip of tea, some shot out his nose, making him snort. They both laughed even more.

They're nuts. This cult is crazy. I need to get out.

"Sorry, but that was funny!" Nafasi said, gaining control of himself.

"What did Ian do to you?" Nafasi asked. "I know he had been looking for you because I asked him to. I know he found you squatting in a mansion in the woods—surrounded by natural beauty, of course. We seek it out like a drug. Plus, we tend to avoid humans. I know he told you about this place, that the Hill View Hotel was gorgeous with very few people. So far, all true. I know he took a phone from you, that you yourself had stolen. He took the phone to protect you because it was possibly being tracked. And I know you're both here now, safe, living in paradise."

It was Tia's turn to swallow hard, shocked by Nafasi's explanation.

"*Safe?* I was almost killed on my way here!" Tia shouted, angry and confused by the conversation.

"Well, yes, that was very unfortunate. Tom Jordisk is the co-owner of the Center and is in charge of security. He takes this responsibility very seriously, especially now. He said someone has been watching us—spying—and I think he confused you with someone else. Then he overreacted, which Tom is inclined to do," Nafasi said, with a casual shrug.

"So, it's okay that he, a man, can't control his emotions and almost killed me? But I, a woman, need to control my anger about being assaulted. Do you understand how fucked up that is? Did he sign The Pledge?" Tia snapped in anger.

"Mr. Jordisk has a lot of things going on. He struggles," Dr. Aufseridish added.

"I don't know how long you have been here, Tia, nor how you grew up or who raised you. I know you were in the foster system in Georgia. I have no idea what memories you have. Under normal circumstances, I would be very eager to hear. I love a good origin story. I know how hard it can be for us. But with July flying by and the 14th just two days away, we don't have time. I will ask the Doc and Ian to explain the situation and you can decide if you have anything productive to contribute, okay?" Nafasi asked.

What the fuck does that even mean?

He looked at Tia as though expecting a response but she stayed silent.

Nafasi continued. "Or you can just hang out by the pool listening to old angry music. I love this old heavy metal. It's like, what were people so angry about in the 80s? Or 90s punk! What was so bad in the 90s, right? It's all so funny."

"Maybe they were pissed off that no one was doing anything to head off the catastrophes that were coming from pollution and space debris," Tia snapped, infuriated.

"Tia, let's calm down and get serious now. Your eyes are jet black and so is your hair. You only eat one meal a day, you heal very fast, you're strong and probably have way keener senses tha—"

Tia jumped at a loud cracking noise that echoed across the hills, gardens, and the terraced lawn. The bullet went straight into Nafasi's head. His eyes opened wide as his neck violently snapped into his shoulder.

Tia slid out of her chair and under the table. The doctor had done the same. Dr. Aufseridish looked at Tia and the terror Tia felt was reflected in her eyes.

"Was that a fucking gunshot?" Tia hissed

Seventeen

Dr. Aufseridish shook her head, eyes wide with shock. Nafasi's body slid out of the chair and crumpled on the ground. A small pool of blood formed just four feet away from Tia. She squeezed her eyes shut in horror.

I didn't trust the guy but I certainly did not want him killed!

A man came up behind her on his hands and knees; Tia jumped so hard she hit her head on the table. He put his finger to his lips, indicating they should stay quiet. For as black as her hair was, his skin was almost the same color.

He stared at Nafasi for a few seconds and then indicated that they should follow him. He ducked down and ran quickly to the labyrinthine garden entrance. Dr. Aufseridish and Tia ran after him as he led them through the maze to the back door of the main building. Once inside, Tia exhaled loudly and followed the swiftly moving man down a long hallway, then another. They finally arrived at a door. He knocked, and it was quickly opened.

When they entered the large room, Tia understood why this was the meeting location: no windows. The walls were covered with pink and white floral wallpaper and old-fashioned elaborate chandeliers hung from the ceiling. Tia wondered if the dark, ornate fireplace had been renovated to look old or had been preserved. There were several people in the room, but no furniture. Tia recognized many faces from the party. Ian was there, talking with the young men he had been sitting with at the party. Tia leaned back against a wall near the huge fireplace, trying not to be seen.

"Is everyone accounted for? Here or in the other safe room?" The man she had followed asked the room.

Many people said yes or mumbled concerns.

"Well, Elizabeth?" He singled out a woman in the crowd.

"Yes, yeah, all accounted for, except for Naf," a woman responded. Tia could not tell which woman said it.

"Doc, what happened? Was that a gunshot? Everyone ran here just like we were trained to do. Where is Nafasi?" someone demanded.

"It seems that Nafasi may have been shot. It's unbelievable, but I think that is what happened," Dr. Aufseridish said with tears in her eyes. "We were having breakfast, joking around, laughing. He was explaining the situation to Tia and then *bam*, a shot from who knows where hit him in the head! He might be dead!"

Might? He is dead. The doctor must be in shock. His head was almost blown off.

"Yaman, you're in charge of security, what do we do? Whoever shot Nafasi, could they be coming for us?" another woman asked. Tia recognized her as the one who said she smelled at the party.

"We have drones out searching the property. We should know soon but with the unstable internet and electricity, it could take some time," Yaman—the man who had led Tia and the doctor to the safe room—replied. His voice was a calm, deep baritone. "And Mr. Jordisk will be doing a perimeter search."

"We should have left! Why did we stay?" another woman asked the room. She was wearing a pantsuit and Tia thought she looked more like a staff member than a guest.

"Because Naf asked us to stay. Because he had a plan to find the truth," another woman snapped. "We agreed to the plan. We agreed to stay. We knew it was dangerous."

Tia thought she looked like the woman who had been wearing the coral blue bathing suit at the party. Today, she was wearing a pink and black workout outfit; the gunshot must have interrupted her yoga class.

There was a loud knock on the door—three quick knocks, three with a slower interval, and finally, three faster ones. Yaman moved swiftly to the door and opened it.

The man from the party with long dreadlocks walked in. He walked toward Yaman and spoke in a strong Caribbean accent, his voice loud enough for the room to hear. He was wearing sunglasses.

"Internet and cameras are back up. We can't find any humans on the property. Tom is doing a thorough perimeter check for drones, humans, or any other kind.

Just stay here and be patient. We will get this sorted out. Doc, please come with me. We took Naf to the medical ward," Dreadlocks said.

"Of course," Dr. Aufseridish said, rushing to follow Dreadlocks out of the room.

Yaman called out to a woman with thick curly red hair, wearing a stylish white tennis outfit, including a retro terrycloth headband and wrist warmers. Tia remembered seeing her at the party too.

"You're in charge of monitoring the door, Elizabeth. Only open it to the code knock until I come back with the okay to leave."

"Of course, Ya. I will stay right here until you come back," she replied, moving closer to the door.

Tia watched Yaman leave the room. Elizabeth locked the door behind him.

People milled around, clustering in groups. The good-looking fashionistas huddled together, while many regular-looking people—Tia thought they must be staff—clumped into smaller groups. The DJ from the party walked between groups, her long yellow hair swishing as she moved. She was shorter than most people in the room, despite her funky platform sneakers. She was wearing huge aviator sunglasses.

Some of the young men sat on the floor in the middle of the room, with their legs stretched out in front of them, leaning back on their elbows. They looked as casual as they had sitting on the wall near the pool.

Tia counted six dazzling fashionistas that seemed like very wealthy guests; six young cool people, including the DJ; and twelve people that looked like staff, dressed in pantsuits, gardening clothes, and other uniforms. She wondered if Wai and Brenda were in the other safe room Yaman had referenced when he asked if everyone was accounted for.

"Are you okay?" Ian asked, startling Tia out of her accounting.

He was standing right next to her, leaning on the wall. She had not heard him approach, distracted by the din of people talking and their loud anxious heartbeats. "What do you care?"

"You saw Naf get shot, right?" Ian asked. "Who fucking shoots people anymore? Who has a gun? It seems like an insult, right? An insult to the hundreds of millions shot on July 14. Did we learn nothing? We all saw enough gun violence for a lifetime—*several* lifetimes. It must have been terrible to see Naf get shot."

"Yes, it was shocking. Terrifying. Just like when I got jumped walking here," Tia snarled. "You are a lying sack of shit. Fuck off."

"What happened to you was bad, really bad, but shooting someone? That's despicable. Has anyone been shot in the last five years? And what are you talking about? When did I lie? I had no idea you were going to get mugged," Ian said, sounding offended.

"I was not mugged. I had nothing to take, and nothing was taken. I was jumped from behind, had my head cracked open, got a concussion, and was burned all over. I was assaulted by a psychopath that lives here, in this fucked-up cult," Tia hissed.

"Cult?" Ian slid down the wall into a sitting position. "You think this is a cult? I mean, I guess maybe. But I have been living and working with Nafasi for almost five years and he has never asked me for money. I think cult leaders want money and power, isn't that how they work?" Ian wondered out loud. "And people don't steal or scam anymore. Sure, they might take some necessities, like food or a phone, but it's not out of greed. I don't think those evil cults exist anymore. Or those Christian televangelist frauds. Either a lot of those people had guns or they are living a different life now."

"I don't know. I don't care," Tia snapped, wanting him to leave. As soon as they got the all-clear, she planned to grab Clorox and leave this bizarre and dangerous hotel forever.

But what if whoever shot Nafasi is still out there? What if they just left the grounds and are in town? I might be stuck here for some time. Fuck! I'm sure cops or those federal agents will come back and ask a lot of questions, I mean, a person was shot! The media will come as well. Ian got me into this situation. I wish he would fuck off!

"A gun with a bullet. I thought guns were gone forever, to the same place as desktop computers, combustion engines, single-use plastic, gas ovens, drift nets, palm oil, and factory farms. The trashcans of history. I hope this was a fluke and not the start of that spiraling stupidity. Everyone wants a gun for safety and suddenly no one is safe from a gun. I will leave for Europe if we start that bullshit again," Ian said.

Tia glanced at his handsome face. This was the kind of talk that made her open up to him in Deep Creek. His warm, earnest voice and conversation reminded Tia of their previous talk.

The talk that led her to the Center in the first place.

Eighteen

At first, Tia had been shocked and uncharacteristically scared when she found him at her forest mansion, sitting on her deck in her favorite chair, calmly drinking a beer. With his thick brown hair, light green eyes, and dark skin, she thought he looked part Italian or maybe Indian or Pakistani, but the green eyes threw her off.

"Get out! I found this place first," she said with more bravery than she felt. Still, she was also overcome with sadness, knowing that even if he left, she would have to move on too. He could sneak back or tell someone she was squatting.

He ruined her paradise. She lashed out.

"Get. The. Fuck. Out," she screamed, throwing his half-full bottle of beer at him. He easily deflected the bottle with his hand, sending it flying over the deck rail.

"Easy, easy. I'll leave tomorrow. I promise. I'm just tired and this view is spectacular," he said in a voice that had a slight Southern twang. "I'm a sucker for a sunset almost as much as I like to watch the sunrise. Birds and bats and other creatures go about their lives with not a concern in the world, at least none from us. Please, let's just sit here. I'll leave in the morning, okay? I signed The Pledge. I live by The Pledge," he responded calmly.

"But you broke in here!" Tia yelled, but even she could hear her tone mellowing out. She liked people that unabashedly appreciated nature and all its beauty.

"So did you. But let's just forget that. There's more beer in the kitchen," he replied. "Why don't you grab a couple for us? Are you hungry?"

Resigned to accepting a sub-squatter in her home, Tia went into the kitchen and grabbed a few beers, a couple of PB & J sandwiches, and some hummus and fruit she had taken from another house. On the counter sat the remnants of a bag of locally made potato chips she'd swiped the other day and had eaten for breakfast. They were so delicious she had saved some for tomorrow.

Good thing he didn't eat my chips, she thought as she slid a knife into her boot, resentful that this douchebag forced her to arm herself.

She took the food and beers and went out to the deck, sitting in her second favorite chair. As she absorbed the beauty of the view, she allowed it to drain the anger away. She would leave soon and never come back. She would enjoy these last few minutes.

"I'm Ian," he said, opening a beer. "I move around a lot, always looking for a nice, quiet place to just be still and think. This part of Maryland is so beautiful. Who would have guessed, right? I'm originally from New Orleans. It's lovely there too, but in a different way. The swamps covered in mist crush me, and the river after it rains looks like hot chocolate. It's so pretty."

Ian took a long swig of beer and nodded his head toward the view.

"But I also love these green hills. I love how the shades of green are different at different times of day and change again when a cloud passes by. After it rains, the green almost vibrates. The mist is different here, the way it clings to the ground. And the smell is divine, so different— and better—than New Orleans," Ian continued.

"Yes, it's stunning and I'm very, very sad I need to leave since you have ruined it," Tia snapped.

"You don't have to leave! Seriously, I will leave in the morning. Maybe I can find another spot like this, or better," Ian said, looking intensely at Tia.

"I have been to many houses around here and there are none like this. There are fantastic houses and there are empty houses, but I haven't found any that are both empty and fantastic. Not like this," Tia said sadly.

"What's your name?" Ian asked.

"Tia," she replied with a shrug, deciding it did not make any difference if she told him.

"Nice to meet you. This is a great house. Being a product of the foster system, I've lived in a lot of houses and apartments all over the city and suburbs. The place I bartended closed temporarily during the pandemic and then permanently after the shooting. So, I just started wandering around. I'm looking for a place I want to stay." Ian gazed at the lake. "There is so much natural beauty in the world, it's hard to decide where to stay put."

Tia had been enjoying the view but looked at Ian in surprise. She had grown up very similarly. Sure, there are millions of kids in the foster system now because of the shooting, but she and Ian were orphans before. Life was very different then and it was a total crap-shoot as to where a kid would end up. Now there were far more orphans but also far more kindness.

Memories of her youth flashed through Tia's mind. Generally, she preferred to not think about it. She would prefer to forget the fear that descended on America on March 15, 2020, as events and flights were canceled and people were advised to go home and stay there. The government said don't go out, but if you must, wear a mask. Don't talk to anyone who didn't live with you. Washing your hands and everything you touched—including groceries, bottles, and cash—became the norm. There were constant images on the news of hospitals overflowing, body bags, people on respirators, and so much death. Tia thought that she would get a few weeks off work and the government would get it under control and it would pass, but it did not. Death came in waves, with hot spots moving from city to city and country to country.

"You were in New Orleans during the pandemic?" Tia asked him. "Even though your bar was closed?"

"Yep," he replied. "And for the shooting."

"I worked in fast food and my restaurant opened during the pandemic," Tia said.

She'd been grateful to go back to work, deemed an essential front-line worker. She preferred to be busy, talking to colleagues and making money, rather than sitting at home, worrying. Even if social distancing and sanitizing were annoying, she respected that food was critical and fast food was comforting. She knew that sitting in a bar drinking for fun was considered too much risk for many Americans; that part of the hospitality sector took a big hit. Even though she was young and healthy and not personally scared of the virus, Tia knew healthcare was being pushed to the brink. Lost jobs and income increased stress levels, and everyone was on edge. Thousands of people were dying every day, leaving loved ones behind to mourn. It was a scary time that would become terrifying.

Tia was at work in a suburb of Atlanta on July 14, working the small pandemic lunch rush. She flinched when she heard gunshots going off in the distance and close by, in the neighborhood behind the parking lot. Tia and her colleagues, accustomed to active shooter drills at school, had dropped to the floor. Everyone instinctively kept quiet; another lesson from the fucked-up world they lived in.

Tia, neck cramping from the awkward position, thought they'd be okay. Well, until a gun went off right outside the drive-thru window. A young cashier screamed bloody murder and ran into the back of the restaurant. A cook put his hands over his ears and kept yelling, "Oh my God" as he followed her back to the walk-in fridge where they barricaded themselves inside. One crew member ran out the back door.

Tia crept to the drive-thru window and peered into the car to find a woman slumped down in the driver's seat, a small hole in her forehead; blood dripped down her face.

The idling cars in the drive-thru lane quickly drove off. One drove over the curb so hard a hubcap flew off. Another crashed through the manicured bushes next to the menu board. Two cars almost collided, in their rush to get away from the nearby gunfire. Tia flinched as another shot exploded close by. With that, she too ran to the walk-in refrigerator.

They speculated in loud whispers what they thought was happening, perhaps a drug or gang-related shootout at the houses behind the restaurant or maybe a mass shooting at the Walmart across the road. They prayed that none of the shooters would enter the restaurant. They jumped around and hugged to stay warm inside the freezer. Tia pulled out large garbage bags that they put on like parkas to avoid frostbite and hypothermia.

Tia kept repeating, "I fucking hate guns. Always have. The weapon of cowards!"

Conversely, her coworker said, "I wish I had my gun. If anyone comes through that door, I would be able to blow their fucking head off!"

After an hour, they worried about the oxygen and carbon dioxide levels, and slowly crept out, hunkering low.

Peeking over the counter and looking out the large front window, they agreed that things looked calm and quiet. Due to the virus, there were very few cars on the road, but still, a few managed to have crashed into each other. There were no people to be seen; Tia assumed that, like them, they took cover and sheltered in place. But there were also no sirens. Tia dialed 9-1-1 to report the dead woman in the drive-thru but she got a busy signal.

"Hello, Tia? You there?" Ian asked.

Tia shook her head and watched Ian take a swig of beer; thankful he interrupted the dreadful memories of that day. "Sorry, just got lost in thought. I grew up in the foster system as well. I think it's different now—in some ways better—since the shooting. I hope so anyway."

"I don't know about that. There are so many orphans now. Kids without parents, missing their parents. I fear many will get lost in the system. Kids do better with parents," Ian said.

Tia just shrugged. Nothing she could do about it.

I have never touched a gun. I did not contribute to space debris. I never had enough stuff to contribute to pollution. I've never been on a plane or owned a car. I avoided the common foster kid age-out trap of jail or pregnancy. The new foster kids are not my problem or concern.

"Let's drink to them. Let's hope they make it," Ian said, tapping his beer bottle against Tia's.

"Okay, to the new foster kids. May they make it out okay," Tia replied.

"How old were you when you went into the system?" he asked.

Tia thought he was being nosey, but she hadn't had a real conversation with anyone since she left her foster dad's house four years ago, and certainly not about the foster system.

"I went to my first foster family when I was around four. At least that's the first one I remember," she replied.

"Wow, you did grow up in it. Do you remember your parents at all?" Ian asked.

"Nope. Not a thing. I don't even know who I stayed with before the Campbell's. Some of the social workers said I blocked it out because it was too painful." Tia shrugged and took a sip of beer.

"Common foster kid story, sadly. Or at least what we are told. I was with my grandmother until I was six and then went into the system when she died. I have no memories of my parents. My grandmother had no interest in them and acted like they never existed. She said my mother overdosed on drugs at seventeen leaving me, a three-month-old, for my grandmother to raise. She seemed to resent it. How many families were you with?" Ian asked.

"Several. I got bullied a lot at homes and at school. I had a couple of good years with an elderly couple. They were shut-ins and on government checks, but they did not give a shit about me and my foster sister so we had it okay. Then the old lady had a stroke and I was back to homes with too many kids and shitty schools. It was awful. But then this woman took me in. She was a party girl and out every night. She forgot I was there unless she needed booze or food or to be picked up from a bar. She taught me to drive her car. She took off for days. I could skip school and do what I wanted—it was good. But then one day she brought home a guy. He was the manager at a place she frequented," Tia continued. She had never told anyone this story and was enjoying herself.

"Oh shit, that does not sound good," Ian said sympathetically.

"I expected the worst. I assumed he would be annoyed and kick me out or come on to me but nope, he was super nice. The woman, Sheila, left for several weeks. We thought she might be dead. The guy, Rick, got me a job at Taco Bell to help cover the bills Sheila had been paying. He helped me lie about my age. We just went along. Neither of us had a car so we walked everywhere, ate meals together, watched movies, and worked. She came back a few times and tried to just blend in like she never left. One time she left and did not return. I quit school at sixteen and worked full-time. Rick helped me get promotions. He taught me how to threaten to claim discrimination because of my disability if I did not get a raise or promotion," Tia laughed at the memory. "It was funny because we knew it was probably my age holding me back, but the disability threat worked. Or maybe I did deserve the promotions. Anyway, I was the store manager when I left Taco Bell at nineteen. Rick encouraged me to get my GED and take some community college finance classes. He was a good guy," Tia said. She had not thought so much about Rick in years.

"What disability?" Ian asked.

"I have aniridia. I was born without irises. I just have a sensitivity to light and some minor problems but my eyes look strange, so I have been bullied about it. Rick taught me to not be discriminated against because of it," Tia explained.

"Interesting. I know a couple of people with eyes like yours and they like them fine as they are," Ian said.

No way he knows 'people'—plural—with my condition. This guy is full of shit.

Tia looked at Ian with disbelief in her eyes. She knew she had an extremely rare condition.

"Yep, and they love nature. I met them at an old abandoned hotel on top of a gorgeous hill in Pennsylvania. I was there once when there were just a few people and once when it was empty. I think it's mostly abandoned. There is a little town and then up, up, up a hill is the old hotel. It's called the Hill View Hotel. Three different words. It has fantastic views and gardens and it's just one of the most divine places I have ever seen. This area is really nice, but that spot is paradise—you'd love it. There are so many critters everywhere: raccoons, skunks, gophers, chipmunks, deer, bears, bats, big cats, every kind of mid-Atlantic bird. More wildlife than here because so few people live in that town or on that hill. I mean, this area is isolated, but just three miles away is a busy road with tourists," Ian said.

"That sounds nice," she responded, thinking maybe she'd go at some point. "Watching wildlife rebound since the shooting has been awesome. No hunting or trapping or cattle grazing has started to rebalance nature and entire ecosystems. Like it's supposed to be."

The sun was setting and the frogs, katydids, and crickets created a symphony of summer evening songs.

"The Hill View Hotel is special," Ian said, before downing his beer. "After the shooting and during the pandemic, I visited state and national parks. Figured we were all going to die anyway, I mean, were the others going to come back? Where was Rex? I signed The Pledge but knew that was no guarantee of anything. Might as well spend my time alive in nature," he continued.

Tia just nodded her head in agreement. It was pretty much what she had done since she quit Taco Bell and said goodbye to Rick. She took odd jobs or worked in fast food for a bit but quit when she felt the need to be alone and in nature. One time, she was hitchhiking and asked the driver to stop by the side of the highway near a particularly lovely forest. She just got out of the car and walked into the woods and stayed there for a few glorious days and nights.

"Do you have a phone?" Ian asked, pulling Tia out of her memories.

"Yes, why?" Tia asked.

"Can I check something? I need to see how to get to Wallops in southern Virginia. I need to head there next. A few years back, I met a guy that sometimes pays me to track down people for him. Since the shooting, he works to reunite missing people and relatives. He wants me to head to Wallops but I lost my phone," Ian explained.

"Uh-huh, okay," Tia said, handing him her phone.

Ian worked on the phone for a minute and smiled. Without taking his eyes off the screen, he said, "This is not your phone, Tia. Did the elderly woman that this phone belongs to give it to you?"

"She left it on a park bench. I picked it up. I'm surprised it still works. She should have shut the account down by now. Whatever," Tia said nonchalantly.

It's not stealing. I found it. At least I'm making use of it and it didn't end up in a landfill. Making phones with all those metals and minerals is highly polluting. It should not be cast away like it's nothing. Nature already sacrificed to provide it; I'm appreciating that sacrifice.

"You could have returned it to her," Ian said, still working on the phone.

"Look, fireflies!" Tia said, excited to point them out and eager to change the subject. "Remember when they were heading to extinction? I'm so happy they're back."

They sat in silence for a while, enjoying the warm evening air and looking for the glow.

"I bet it's freezing out here in the winter. But it's also probably incredibly radiant covered in snow and ice," Ian said. "Beautiful, just like your unusual black eyes."

Tia detected something in his tone she did not like. It was as though he was flirting, but Tia was not sure. Flirting or not, her defenses were triggered. "I'm going to bed. You'd better not be here in the morning." She stood up to leave.

"Here, wait, take this," Ian said, handing her a small piece of paper. "If you ever want to see paradise, check it out."

The words *Hill View Hotel, Central Road,* were written on it, but nothing else.

"Where is it?" Tia asked.

"Janssen, Pennsylvania," Ian replied. "It's been nice talking to you. You don't meet that many people that aged out of the system and are normal."

"That's true. Good night, Ian. You'd better not be here in the morning," Tia reiterated, pointing a finger at him and then in the direction of the road.

In the house, she did not turn on any lights as she went about her normal routine. She went into the master bedroom and put the phone on the universal charger before heading to her plain little out-of-the-way bedroom across the house. She made sure the door was locked and, for added security, moved a heavy table and chair in front of it. At least it would slow Ian down if he tried to get in.

Shit, he could have been texting friends about a woman alone in the woods when I gave him the phone! I'm an idiot! Or maybe I'm just out of practice when it comes to dealing with people. Of course, he did disarm me with his love of nature and claim he adheres to The Pledge. Crime is almost nonexistent and people are kinder since the shooting. I'm sure he's okay.

Tia undressed but hesitated before she crawled into bed.

She pulled the knife out of her boot and put it under her pillow.

Just to be sure.

Nineteen

"**Y**ou are a lying sack of shit, Ian, and you know it!" Tia said, feeling her face getting hot at the memory of how he had deceived her back in Maryland, though she knew full well her skin would stay its normal pale color.

Ian just shrugged, making Tia angrier.

"You said this place was empty—abandoned! There are dozens of people here and you clearly live here or vacation here. You were very aware of this crowd when you lied to me." She lowered her voice, trying not to attract attention.

These are Ian's people, after all. Who knows what they will do to me?

"But you can't be angry. Is it not gorgeous? Is it not paradise? The Center is environmentally sustainable. Nature abounds! This is the best place for our kind to live. You should be thanking me. Most everyone I bring here does," Ian responded calmly. "Sometimes, it *is* empty. Especially at this time of year."

Tia's mouth hung open in shock.

"What do you mean 'everyone you bring here?' Orphans?" Tia felt her blood run cold.

"Did Nafasi not explain? He locates us. We're all on the lookout, of course, but Nafasi is very good at it.

Then he sends me or one of the other guys to go and find you and direct you here, one way or another. If they are alone, like you were, and most are, it's pretty easy. We are all out there, looking for something. For most of us, the planet is so sublime and full of life, and we have to be out in nature. And, because of our issues, like your eyes, we prefer to avoid humans," Ian said. "We live in balance with nature here. Most of us are vegan. Most of us only eat once a day. Why do you look so confused?" Ian asked, alarmed by the look on Tia's face.

"Humans? What do you mean? We're all humans!" Tia said, loud enough for several heads to turn their way.

"Oh shit. Was Nafasi shot before you had the talk?" Ian asked, seriously alarmed.

Just then, the code knock drew everyone's attention and Elizabeth rushed to open the door. In walked the man with dreadlocks, and two other men with perfectly coifed silver hair and matching beards. They were followed by the pale creep that Tia thought almost killed her.

Tia's heart started to race.

The pale creep stomped into the room with his fists clenched and went directly to Elizabeth. They were all gathered around her, speaking quietly. Tia could not hear a word due to their whispering and her own thumping heart.

"The pale guy, Mr. Jordisk, looks angry. I wonder if he figured out who shot Nafasi. He would have been the one to find out—he's the only one that can do a full perimeter search super-fast. This place is huge," Ian whispered to Tia.

Suddenly, all eyes turned toward them.

Mr. Jordisk rushed over to Tia and put his hand around her throat so quickly that neither Tia nor Ian could react. He pulled her up from her sitting position and slammed her head against the wall. Tia grabbed at his arms, trying to make him release her.

"This will not solve anything, Tom," one of the bearded me called out, but without any particular urgency. "Release her before you kill her. We need to ask her questions."

His pale light brown eyes stared into Tia's black ones with pure rage. He put his face within an inch of hers and inhaled very loudly. He opened his mouth wide like he was about to bite her face.

"We don't have time for this, Tom," Dreadlocks said, trying to pull Tom off Tia. "Seriously, stop it now!"

The creep slowly closed his mouth and put his face so close to Tia's that their eyelashes touched. She felt a sensation of burning before he violently smashed her head against the wall again.

She blacked out.

Twenty

Tia tried to open her eyes. She moved her head slightly and flinched when the back of her skull pressed to the floor.

"Stay down," Ian whispered. "Stay asleep."

He placed a cold towel on her forehead and gently turned her chin to press an ice pack against the back of her head.

"I'm not sure what is happening but it's best to not get up until Mr. Jordisk leaves, okay?' Ian whispered into her ear as he adjusted the ice pack.

Tia squeezed her eyes shut and tried to calm her thumping heart.

I need to think about waterfalls and sunsets and free tigers—beautiful things that will make me heal fast because I need to get the fuck out of here before that psycho kills me. Fuck Ian for tricking me into coming here, even if he is being nice right now. I definitely can't trust him. What about all that crazy shit he said? Did he say I wasn't human?

"Okay, he's gone. Follow my lead," Ian whispered. He placed his hands under Tia's body and scooped her up as he stood, cradling her in his arms. He easily carried her as though she was a baby and not a full-grown, 5-foot-7-inch muscular woman.

"She is still out of it. Not sure what Mr. Jordisk was upset about. I found her. She seems completely harmless. She was with Nafasi when he was shot, so she did not shoot him! I'm taking her to see Doc. She needs medical help," Ian said as he walked slowly toward the door.

Tia kept her eyes shut and her head pressed against Ian's chest.

"That sounds good, Ian. Tom is wound up so tight right now and Nafasi being shot seems to have sent him over the edge. He'll be okay when he finds out what happened," Elizabeth said.

Tia could tell by her voice she was getting closer.

"Here, let me get the door. Be careful, Ian. We still have no idea who shot Naf," Elizabeth said.

"Thanks. I'll be back," Ian replied.

With her eyes still shut, Tia heard the door close behind them. Ian started to jog. She could feel his heartbeat through his shirt. Her head jostled against his chin a couple of times as he quickened his pace.

"Okay. Put me down," Tia squawked from her throbbing throat, squirming around.

"Wait until we're outside. There are cameras everywhere. Be sure to look unstable when I put you down," Ian instructed.

A minute later, they exited the building through an inconspicuous fire door.

Close to noon, it was already scorching. Ian softly set Tia down and she swooned, almost hitting the ground before he grabbed her.

"Whoa! Shit! I thought you were overacting," Ian said, picking Tia back up. "I guess we are going to the medical floor."

"No! Ian, put me down! It's just so hot. I need water. I won't be locked up in the medical room again. I'll claw your eyes out first!" Tia hissed, her throat screaming with each word. "Take me to the maze."

"You know it's not a real maze. The shrubs and trees and paths make it seem like one, but once you know it, it's not a maze. Just another garden," Ian calmly explained as he carried Tia. He took her to one of the shady picturesque benches and put her down.

Sitting in the shade, Tia felt better. She took a few deep breaths. Her throat ached with each one. She rubbed her throat gently. Her head was feeling much better, but her throat still felt as though it had been nearly crushed.

"I'm going to go to the pool bar and get some water," Ian said. "Stay here."

Tia lay down on the bench, willing her throat to heal quickly. She needed to get Clorox and get far away. She was creating an escape plan when Ian reappeared, startling Tia so much that she almost fell off the bench.

"Here you go," he said, handing Tia a reusable water bottle that had the words "Hill View Hotel Center" printed on it.

Tia sat up and downed half the bottle in one huge, painful gulp.

Fuck it. Honesty is the best policy. And I'm in a hurry.

"I'm leaving, but first, I need you to go to the room I was staying in and let my cat out. I'll stay here. Run and do that. Lead her here. Go now," Tia said in a whisper while holding her throat, though the pain was lessening.

Ian sat down on the bench next to her and slowly nodded.

"What the fuck, Ian! Go!" Tia urged.

"I understand why you want to go, but I'm not sure it's a good idea," he replied, giving her a sidelong glance.

"Are you kidding? That insane creep almost killed me right in front of your friends and colleagues! No one said a word about assault or calling the cops or attempted murder or the fucking Pledge! And you were the only one that helped me! There is something seriously wrong with these people and I'm not giving Tom another chance to kill me!" Tia hissed, which caused her to cough, hurting her bruised throat even more.

"It's so strange. Mr. Jordisk seems to think you shot Nafasi. People trust him when it comes to security so maybe they all think it's a possibility," Ian mused.

"I was with Nafasi when he was shot! I did not shoot him! Why do you call him 'Mr. Jordisk?'" Tia asked.

"He wanted to be called 'Mr. Jordisk.' He kind of co-owns this place. He and Nafasi are business partners. I guess I work for both of them. Naf is more laid back. Mr. Jordisk is more uptight. We generally use short versions of each other's names or nicknames, but all the staff call him 'Mr. Jordisk,'" Ian explained. "This situation is so odd. We need to figure out what to do. Maybe we should go find Doc. Get you checked out and find out what is going on."

A movement caught Tia's eye.

Am I hallucinating? Do I have another concussion? Or is something small moving under that shrub?

"Have you ever seen him attempt to kill a guest or staff member before?" Tia asked to keep Ian focused on her and the conversation and not the movement.

"No, no, can't say I have," Ian replied with a small laugh.

In the shade at the bottom of a somewhat far-off shrub, another movement.

"Whatever. He's a violent piece of shit. Please, go release my cat. Bring her here," Tia begged.

"Okay, fine. But stay right here," Ian said.

"I'm not going anywhere without my cat. I'm not exactly sure what the room number is. Shit, I think it was on the fifth floor. Maybe?" Tia said, becoming distressed.

"Don't worry. I know where they keep people during the transition," Ian said as he stood up. "I'll find it. Does it bite?"

"Yes, but only if you try to touch her. Just let her out," Tia said, trying to keep her eyes off the moving shadow so Ian wouldn't notice. "During transition? What the fuck does that mean? Whatever! Just go!"

"Okay," Ian said as he rushed off.

Tia sat on the bench for two minutes to be sure he did not come back. It was very quiet, except for the buzz of bees and other insects and, occasionally, the squawk of a bird. Way off in the distance, she heard a goat bleating. She was not only listening for Ian's return but for Tom or anyone else. When she felt it had been quiet for long enough, she left the bench and silently crept around the vicinity, looking for people and cameras.

When she felt confident that she was alone for the moment, she walked toward the little shadow under the shrub and bent down.

Two green eyes peered up at her.

"You ready to get the fuck out of here, Clorox?" Tia asked as the cat got up, stretched, and walked away.

They walked along in silence. Clorox led the way, moving quickly along the paved walkway, which turned into dirt paths leading to the forest.

"Do you know how to get down the hill and into town without going near the road?" Tia whispered. "I mean, this forest is pretty dense."

The cat looked over her shoulder at Tia and blinked but did not stop walking. She almost looked bored.

"Okay, I guess going into town would be stupid. And I would not mind just getting lost in this pretty forest, but we need to get far away fast, and these are their woods. Oh, and there are tigers out here! Fucking tigers!" Tia said with a scratchy voice, looking around for danger.

Twenty-One

Four hours later, Tia was sitting on a rock filling the water bottle from a bubbling creek. She splashed water on her face and neck. It still hurt but felt much better than it did even an hour ago.

The woods were cool and dark, with moss growing everywhere, its particular shade of green popping among all the other greens of leaves, vines, and shrubs. The tall trees sang when a breeze moved their foliage and thick branches together. She could hear insects munching on leaves and birds digging around for worms. The calm sounds of nature and the earthen aroma made Tia momentarily forget the terrible situation she was in. Clorox sat several feet away on another rock, her tiny pink tongue scooping up water.

A branch snapped, making Tia's blood run cold.

Clorox heard it too and sprinted for a hiding place before Tia could even stand up. She ducked as she scurried toward a clump of bushes and squatted down, listening.

Tigers?

Suddenly Ian entered the clearing next to the creek. He just stared at the water for a moment before his eyes seemed to fix on the rock Tia had recently been sitting on.

"Do you say creek or crick?" Ian asked.

Tia stayed still, holding her breath behind the dense shrubs.

Has he seen me? How?

"Tia, I know you are hiding in those bushes. Come out. Tell me which pronunciation you prefer. The correct one or the provincial one. I mean, I'm fine with them both, God knows Louisianans have their own way of talking," Ian said, switching to a southern bayou accent. "But the Pennsylvanian accent is pretty distinct. Come out, I have some food and your bag," he added in his regular voice, holding up Tia's backpack. "Your cat was not in the room when I got there, as you well know."

Tia stayed silent and hidden, her racing heart making a thumping sound she hoped he couldn't hear.

"Come on, Tia. We need to talk. I realize this place must seem terrifying to you. You were attacked on your way here. And you didn't get the regular introduction talk and time to think and accept the truth. Then you saw Nafasi get shot just a few feet away from you. I understand that you are freaked out and scared shitless. But let's talk. We need a plan," Ian said in a very calm and soothing voice, his eyes still on the creek

Fuck this guy. He's a manipulator. How did he even find us? Don't trust him, remember he gets people to come here 'one way or another,' whatever that means.

"I can just keep following you. It's what I do. Naf or someone else from our group tasks me with tracking our kind down. I'm very good at my job, so just save us both time. Come out and we can talk," he continued.

Our kind?

Tia's curiosity won out.

"Goddammit," Tia said as she walked out of her hiding spot. "What do you mean 'us' and 'our kind' and *how* did you track me in these woods?"

"Hungry?" Ian asked, handing her the backpack.

"Nope, ate this morning. I was having breakfast with Nafasi when he was shot in the head," Tia replied coolly. "How did you track us?"

"I don't know. I just can. I think I see this world kind of like dogs do—a powerful sense of smell and hearing. How do you heal so fast? How do we survive on one meal a day when humans need three?" Ian asked with a dramatic shrug.

"Most people don't need so much food, they just want it," Tia replied, looking in her backpack and finding the canister with the burned plastic things, sunglasses, the ointment, and a few articles of clothing. "And people are much healthier than before the shooting; many eat less, it's called intermittent fasting. It's not that strange. All humans have become more conscientious about consumption. We don't want Rex to come back."

"But we are like athletes—certainly very strong compared to most. We should want and need to eat more, not less," Ian continued.

"Many professional athletes are vegan and do fasting," Tia snapped. "And I'm not that strong. Tom Jordisk almost killed me twice!"

"Well, Mr. Jordsik is stronger than everyone," Ian replied with a strange look on his face.

Clorox emerged confidently walking towards them but then suddenly veered off into the woods and away from the water.

"I need to follow her. Thanks for bringing my backpack. Go back to your 'kind,' okay? I hope I never see you again," Tia said as she went after the cat.

But Ian just followed and kept talking. "What do your strange eyes see?"

"Same stuff everyone does," she replied. "Seriously. Go back to the Center. I know you're following me to bring me back or report me to your boss. But I'm not going back to where I was assaulted … *twice!*"

"I get it. You're not going back. Makes sense. Things are pretty crazy there now anyway. Doc was trying to revive Nafasi so a lot of guests and staff were on the medical floor, making suggestions, praying, whatever. I couldn't tell if it was legit or just wishful thinking," Ian said.

"Wishful thinking. I saw his eyes. He's dead," Tia said, trying to soften her tone. She knew Ian liked and respected Nafasi, even if she didn't.

"You never know. There are all kinds at the Center. Mr. Jordisk was encouraging Doc to do everything she could and ordered the security team to find out where the bullet came from. They said the grounds were clear but who knows what that means. Anyway, that's all I heard," Ian said, following several steps behind Tia.

"I don't care," Tia replied.

"And then something happened with the power and computers again," Ian continued. "I realized I was no help there and came looking for you."

"Whatever. I don't give two shits," she snapped.

"So, you're just blindly following your cat? It'll eventually get dark," Ian said.

"We're fine," Tia called over her shoulder. "Just go back!"

"How do you know the cat isn't leading you back to the Center? Where it ate last? Animals always head for food," Ian said. "Unless it's some kind of special cat?"

A deep growl penetrated the thick woods, making Tia and Ian stop dead in their tracks.

"Shit. Did you know there are tigers out here?" Ian asked in a whisper, his eyes huge with fear.

Tia just nodded her head and started to jog in the opposite direction of the growl.

"I don't think we should run!" Ian whispered, jogging right behind her.

"According to Nafasi, they are old, feeble, and well-fed, so I think we should just get as far as possible from it, whatever it is," Tia whispered back, picking up her pace.

It was difficult to run on the rough terrain. Tia wanted to sprint outright but could not because she had to avoid trees, duck under low branches, and occasionally jump over fallen trunks, all while she kept her eyes on a little gray and white blur hustling through the woods a hundred feet ahead of her.

They jogged for a couple of hours, mostly uphill. Tia figured they were far away from the growl, but it felt good to be moving somewhat fast and not talking. The evening air was cooling down and she was perfectly content to keep increasing the distance between her, the growl, and the Hill View Hotel Center. The forest was so lovely; she looked forward to sleeping under the stars later. But before she slept, she needed to convince Ian to leave.

Lost in her concentration to not trip, lose an eye, keep up with the cat, and strategize, she was shocked when she emerged into a clearing. It was not a meadow, but a mowed grassy field with a large, ugly building.

She came to such an abrupt stop Ian ran into her.

"What the hell?" Ian asked in surprise.

"Shush, Ian," Tia mumbled as she turned and rushed back into the woods. The building gave her the creeps and she wanted to get away from it.

When she was safely concealed in the forest, Tia sat down behind a large tree, opened the water bottle, and took a swig. She could hear Ian walking closer.

"Tia?" Ian called softly. "I know you're here."

If he is such a great tracker, he should be able to find me behind a tree for fuck's sake.

"Why would your cat lead you to that building?" Ian asked, as he moved around the tree and stood over her.

"Why don't you fuck off back to the Hill View Hotel Center? What's it to you anyway? What I do is none of your goddam business!" Tia snapped and took another gulp of water.

The water shot out of Tia's nose when she heard a twig snap. The guy with the long dreadlocks came silently around the tree.

"We would like to know as well, Tia. You being here is *definitely* our business."

Twenty-two

Tia jumped up.

There was a second man, one of the good-looking guys that had been sitting on the wall with Ian at the party and, later, on the floor in the hotel conference room where they sheltered in place.

"Great! Why not just lead them to me, Ian?" Tia chided.

"Technically, we came to them. But these are good people, don't worry. Paul Ekstraterès does research and security." Ian nodded toward the dreadlocked man. "And this is Sebastian. He does tracking, like me."

"Hi Tia, you've had an exciting day. You were with Nafasi when he was shot this morning, attacked by Jordisk, and now you have found our research location. We would like for you to come with us. We can explain what we are doing, and you can explain how you found us, deal?" Paul Ekstraterès asked, with his thick island accent.

Like hell I'm going with them.

"Nope, I'm heading out of town and out of the state right now. You can go about your business, and I will go about mine. I literally could not care less what you are doing." Tia tossed the backpack over her shoulder and started to walk deeper into the woods.

"We were following her cat," Ian said.

"Oh, oh, she has a cat. That explains it," Ekstraterès said, nodding his head.

"Come on, Tia, I'm dying to know what is going on! Let's go in and talk and then you can leave if you want to. How are you not curious?" Ian pleaded.

Tia paused and turned back to the group of men. "What do you mean, 'she has a cat and that explains it?'" Tia asked Ekstraterès.

"The research we are doing is trying to determine where we are from. How long have you had your cat? Did you get it from the pound? Or did it find you? I think it found you. I think it found this place for you," Ekstraterès said, opening his arms wide.

Wait? What? No. I found Clorox. Not the other way around.

"Where are you from?" Tia asked as a distraction while she thought this through.

All of these guys appear to be in great shape. If they are like Ian, running away will not work. Why the fuck did Clorox lead me into this situation? I need to get away. No way I'm going inside that hideous building.

"What do you mean, 'where am I from?'" Ekstraterès asked.

"Okay, I'm from Georgia. Ian says he's from Louisiana. You sound like you're from an island. It's none of your business how long I've had my cat. I'm out of here," Tia said, walking away.

Sebastian laughed and Tia shot him a look that said, "Eat shit."

"Yes, yes, I'm from the West Indies, an island called Nevis. We can't let you leave until our very important experiment is completed. You must stay until at least the 15th, or maybe the 16th, okay? Just a few more days. Come, it's very interesting. We don't have weapons, of course, we believe in The Pledge, but there are three of us and only one of you," Ekstraterès replied. "We don't want to force you, but we will if we must."

Tia looked from Ian to Ekstraterès to the other guy, Sebastian. They all drew nearer, as if on cue. No way she could take them all out or outrun them. She had no choice.

I'm fucked.

Twenty-three

They walked back to the strange building in tense silence. Tia seethed. They claimed they 'believed' in The Pledge and yet they had kidnapped her. Did The Pledge mention kidnapping? Tia could not recall, though she knew for a fact it said to treat everyone and everything with respect and kindness.

This was a violation.

The windowless concrete building reminded her of a federal building, designed in an era where aesthetics were unimportant. Approximately twelve floors high, it had the look of an old-fashioned flour mill.

It should be a crime to build something so ugly in this forest.

As they walked toward a door, movement across the meadow caught her eye. It was getting dark, but the gray and white contrasted enough for Tia to see.

Thanks for leading me back to danger and imprisonment, Clorox.

Sebastian interrupted her angry thoughts as he held the door open. "I've never met someone that has been with us for so long and doesn't accept reality. I mean, it's so *obvious* but she's still in denial. It's strange, right, Ekstra? Have you seen this before?"

"No, it's very unusual. Most are relieved. Tia, follow us and we will show you the roof," Ekstraterès said. "You may have observed many communication problems as of late."

Tia just nodded her head in the affirmative, thinking about the woman who found her after the assault. Was it just this morning that she walked with Caitlin and her dog? Caitlin had said something about the internet being down again. Nafasi said the bus station could not sell tickets. The Center seemed to have constant problems since she got there. Tia often lived off the grid but, from her Taco Bell days, she knew whole systems going down for hours was uncommon.

"Ekstra or Ekstraterès?" Tia asked, stumbling over the pronunciation.

"Lots of foreign names here so we tend to give nicknames to make it easier, and it's a sign of affection, you know, 'cause we are all in the same club," Sebastian explained with a grin. "Like we call Nafasi, 'Naf' and Ekstraterès, 'Ekstra.' Some people call me Sabi."

Tia nodded at Sebastian but directed her question at Ekstra. "So, this town seems to have an internet problem, what of it?"

"Not just this town, the disruptions are happening all over America and the world," Ekstra replied.

Tia shrugged indifferently.

"There have been an extraordinary number of solar flares this month," Ekstra said.

Tia shrugged again.

"Do you understand solar flares?" Ekstra asked Tia intensely. He seemed frustrated by her lack of knowledge and concern, as though he took it personally that she had no interest in solar flares.

They walked through a dark, bland foyer with cement floors. Three hallways shot out from the foyer. One straight in front of them, one to the right, and another to the left. They were wide halls with low ceilings, and it made Tia feel like she was in the basement of an office building.

Ekstra turned to look at Tia as he explained the situation. "There have been an extraordinary number of radiation bursts from the sun. Most are from the magnetic energy created by a sunspot, or the unexpected acceleration of protons and electrons along the sun's surface. Sometimes, for several hours, everything—including solar, gamma, and electromagnetic radiation—is released. Solar flares generally occur too quickly to be seen and are never visible to the naked eye. However, depending on how long it lasts, it can appear as a bright flash if viewed using special instruments, which we have here," Ekstra said.

Tia slowly nodded, indicating she was following him. He did not seem to entirely believe her.

"Tia, solar flares occur when charged particles in the sun's plasma erupt into space, traveling with enormous speed. These flares can increase the effect of solar wind, the force of the particles constantly flowing out of the sun through the solar system, or they can cause a coronal mass ejection, a massive burst of charged particles, and magnetic fields. If a solar flare strikes Earth, it can cause several different effects," Ekstra said slowly, as though he thought his cadence was causing her confusion.

Tia shrugged again. "Okay, but nothing to do with me."

"Tia, it affects all of us. One of the more significant dangers of a solar flare is widespread electrical disruption. When the particles strike the Earth's magnetosphere, they can produce an electrical charge, one strong enough to reach the surface of the planet. When these charged currents encounter electrical grids, it can cause a number of problems. In 1989, a strong solar flare struck North America and shut down the electrical grid of Quebec, causing widespread failures and a blackout that lasted 12 hours," Ekstra elaborated.

"Sucks for the Canadians, but I have no idea what this has to do with me," Tia interrupted.

Ekstra sighed loudly but kept going.

"Okay, you understand that solar flares can disrupt communication systems. The geomagnetic storms caused by a flare striking Earth produce electrical interference high in the atmosphere, affecting radio and other broadcast communication. Depending on the intensity of the flare, this can range from mild static interference to a complete block of communication for the storm's duration. Shortwave communications are particularly vulnerable to disruption since they take advantage of electrical conditions in the Earth's atmosphere to bounce signals across great distances."

Tia changed tactics. She furrowed her brow and nodded her head as though she not only understood but that this was the most fascinating story she had ever heard.

"Okay, then I will tie it to something so resplendent that it will make sense to you," Ekstra said with a smile, seeing through her ruse. "Near the poles, the aurora borealis and aurora australis produce vivid, colorful sky shows at night. These effects are the result of excited particles interacting high in the Earth's atmosphere. The charged particles from a solar flare can drastically increase the effect of these lights in the sky, extending their range and increasing their intensity. During the March 1989 storm, the aurora borealis, typically restricted to Canada and Alaska, was visible as far south as Florida."

I've always wanted to see the Northern lights! I have seen many pictures and live feeds, but what must it be like to be bundled up as the sky explodes with beauty? Okay, he has made this pointless lecture interesting.

"Is that happening again?" Tia asked. "When? I want to see that!"

"Not exactly. And the situation is more dangerous now. While the Earth's atmosphere protects against the radiation from solar flares and mitigates some of their electrical effects, people and objects in orbit have considerably less protection. The International Space Station flies in a low enough orbit that the effects of solar flares are somewhat mitigated, but satellites in high geosynchronous orbit may be harmed. Many satellites contain protection against electrical disruption with built-in Faraday cages, but flares can block signals to and from satellites and, in some rare cases, shut them down completely. This can lead to communication disruptions on Earth, shutting down international telephone links and television satellite feeds," Ekstra explained.

"Okay, that sucks for the astronauts on the Space Station and people streaming or gaming, but it has nothing to do with me. There's almost no space debris now, which must make things better, right? If the atmosphere is mostly clean, maybe the sky is like the one in 1989 and we will get to see the Northern lights!" Tia said enthusiastically.

"No, Tia! You are missing the point," Ekstra said

"Okay," Tia said flatly, getting frustrated again. "We can't communicate. It's okay, Ekstra, we will survive. We've faced worse."

"Unprotected by our planet's magnetic field, particles from a solar storm could deposit charges on satellites' electronics, short-circuiting them and rendering them inoperable. Yes, we lose satellite communications, we lose unnecessary communications like TV, but we also lose all military and civil communications. Drones, aircraft carriers, and ships will not work. No internet. No weather warning systems. No GPS," Ekstra elaborated.

Okay, that sounds more serious.

"Usually, satellites boost their speed to offset the drag of particles that cause them to slow and drift lower, where they would eventually burn up in the atmosphere. This major solar storm has required satellites to be maneuvered back into orbit every few days or be lost. It's difficult. We may lose many permanently, impacting communications for a long time," Ekstra continued, seeming determined to make Tia understand.

"Wait, will this create space debris? Are you worried Rex and the others will come back?" Tia asked, frightened at the thought.

"Yes and no," Ekstra replied, smiling again.

"I don't think this is funny at all," Tia said. "Why is this happening?"

"Good question," Ekstra replied. "Solar flares come from sunspots that pulsate with energy. They're also places from which magnetic flux pours out; those magnetic field lines loop back and reconnect elsewhere on the sun's surface and a flare is ejected from the original sunspot. The number of flares that occur is proportional to the number of sunspots. Those sunspots are most common at the peak of a solar cycle, which occurs every 11 years. Years ago, NASA forecasted the next solar maximum would occur in July 2025; they anticipated about 115 sunspots in July alone. We have already had 115 sunspots and we are not even halfway through July. Communications worldwide have been disrupted and, yes, many satellites are becoming useless pieces of debris, if they are not burning up. Why? It's science and nature and chaos in space!"

"What the fuck?" Tia asked. "And this makes you happy?"

Laughing, Ekstra tossed his dreadlock-covered head back and clapped his hands, seemingly delighted at his own story. "For comparison, the number of sunspots and flares last year was 91, with 274 days without so much as a blemish on the sun."

Tia looked around the room. Everyone seemed engrossed with Ekstra's story. Sebastian nodded his head in agreement or encouragement, while Ian's mouth was slightly ajar as though this was the first he had heard it.

"I'm confused. Why is this good news?" Tia asked.

"We don't just want a spectacular aurora borealis. We *need* it to be dangerous and it is. We knew this month would have the most solar flares recorded to date. There are spontaneous blackouts and communication systems are going down everywhere. This moment in time is what we have waited for—it's what Nafasi, myself, and everyone here has waited for since July 14, 2020." Ekstra's voice rose in excitement.

A shiver ran down Tia's spine.

What the hell does this have to do with the shooting? Why does he sound like a mad scientist, excited about that horrific tragedy and this current dangerous situation?

"Why have you been waiting?" Tia asked.

"So that no one can see what we're doing!" Ekstra said, with a huge smile.

Twenty-four

"Come, I will take you upstairs and it will make more sense," Ekstra said, indicating everyone should follow as he walked down a hallway and to an elevator.

As they approached the elevator Tia saw a large, framed document hanging on the wall. She walked closer to read it in the dim light. It was The Pledge that Kate Stellute asked people to sign before they could go into space with Rex to escape annihilation. It was the promise to behave better. It changed the world. It took a global catastrophe to make the world kind and livable. Hundreds of millions of people had signed it.

Tia felt a wave of relief seeing it and smiled as she quickly read the words she almost knew by heart.

This is how most of us promised to live in space and most of us adopted it here on Earth. Some, because they feared that if they did not, Rex or the others would return. But for many, just because it made the world better. It made us better—me better.

"I bet she would have written it differently now, included more detail," Ekstra said, watching Tia read it.

"She did a great job under enormous pressure and a serious time crunch," Tia responded, annoyed that anyone would criticize Kate's work.

"The elevator is coming," Ekstra said, hearing it arrive.

But before they could enter it, the exterior door opened so hard it slammed against the wall with a loud bang.

Tom Jordisk entered the room in all his pale, muscular blandness, radiating pure rage. Tia ducked behind Ekstra's tall frame and Ian moved to block her.

"Hey, Tom, how is everything?" Ekstra asked calmly, seemingly unbothered by the psychopath's dramatic entrance.

"Fucking mess. Nafasi is dead and his killer is still loose. What the hell is going on here? I told you to take her into custody!" Jordisk demanded in a quiet tone.

Tia's heart raced and she started to shake, her flight or fight instincts kicking in hardcore.

"Come now, Tom, we have her in custody. She's not going anywhere. I was just explaining to her and Ian the incredible situation we are in now. I was about to take them up and show them Nafasi's life's work. Soon, hopefully, it will be an amazing success for him and all of us. It would be the best way to honor Naf," Ekstra said, sounding both excited and sad.

"Don't take her up. At the very least, she might be an infiltrator or spy, working with an entity determined to stop us. Or perhaps she's just a cold-blooded killer working on her own? She does not deserve to see the work being done here. The fucked-up thing is that she is one of us," Jordisk said, getting angrier.

No, I'm nothing like this violent man.

"If she is a moronic fool working for a government agency, or more accurately, being used by a government agency, she may delay and hurt us but, in the end, still benefits from our efforts. She should be killed," Jordisk said, seething with rage.

What the fuck? Me, working with the government? Ha! No way in hell.

"You are too upset, Tom Jordisk. You're not thinking clearly. We know what can happen when you get too emotional. She is with us. We will not let her out of our sight until the experiment is over. She has no way to communicate with anyone else, especially inside these walls. Nafasi thought she was one of us and was excited to welcome her, even if she seemed more confused and reluctant than most. I will put my trust in Nafasi," Ekstra said calmly.

"We have excellent security, both human and otherwise, but she has enormous power, or whomever she is working for does! How did they infiltrate us? How did someone shoot Nafasi dead? She is coming with me, and I will get answers!" Jordisk shouted.

No one spoke or moved.

They are scared of him. They must realize what a violent psychopath he is.

"I want to show her what we are doing. Regardless of who she might be working for, she could get excited and want us to succeed once she understands. I realize you are in charge of security, and we are experiencing a massive security breach, but no one blames you. You will learn the truth and find Nafasi's killer. You just need to calm down and get your energy under control," Ekstra replied, his voice calm and soothing.

"It's like no one cares that Nafasi is dead. Everyone is back to business—guests annoyed that we are still in lockdown, staff complaining because they can't do their work, you calmly 'educating' a murderer," Jordisk said, his mouth a black blur and his skin paling.

"No one cares that Nafasi is dead? I beg to differ. I believe I care the most that Naf is dead, but I know he would want his experiment to go on. Timing is crucial, as you well know. Sebastian, take Ian and Tia up and I will join you soon," Ekstra said, his eyes locked on Jordisk's.

"Sure, but I think they need you up there as well. We have been delayed by Tia for some time now. Please follow me, Tia, Ian," Sebastian said, indicating they should enter the elevator. "They need you up there more than us, Ekstra."

Ian and Tia entered the elevator. Sebastian stood in the doorway, preventing the doors from closing. "Come up, Ekstra. I think Mr. Jordisk should go find Tia's cat. I mean, it led her here. Maybe it knows something. It was out there in the forest watching the building a few minutes ago," Sebastian said.

"What the fuck!" Tia stepped forward but Ian grabbed her arms and Sebastian blocked the door.

"That is a good idea. Go and find it, Tom. That sounds like a security breach and you are head of security," Ekstra said before he smoothly entered the elevator and the doors closed.

Twenty-five

"We need to get away from Tom when he gets like that," Ekstra said, facing the doors. He didn't look at Tia, who was still being restrained by Ian.

"Get your hands off me, Ian!" Tia shouted, jamming her elbows into Ian's stomach.

"Please refrain from violence. We all signed The Pledge, we must adhere to its principles," Ekstra said, still facing the closed doors.

"But kidnapping me, keeping me against my will, and allowing your psychopath to almost kill me, well, that is all okay! Right? Just ignore The Pledge! But when your psychopath turns on you, well then, we'd better adhere to The Pledge! How convenient for you!" Tia shouted as the elevator doors opened.

No one addressed her concerns, they just silently walked out.

They were on what seemed to be the highest floor. Tia looked up and could see the sky. It was not what she expected to see, and it was a bit discombobulating. For a moment, she forgot about Clorox. It was twilight so there were no stars yet. On this level and for many below, there was just one walkway that looped around with a metal railing to prevent a person from falling off the platform. Tia could see clearly across to the opposite side of the room, which was the opposite side of the building. She took a few steps toward the railing and looked down. She could see a huge piece of equipment.

Suddenly, a loud alarm went off, making Tia jump.

"Whoa, no worries, Tia," Ekstra said loudly in his Caribbean accent. "It's a warning to step back as they move the radio telescope up through the hole in the roof. They can send the electromagnetic beam now. It's a good warning, not a dangerous one. Step back and watch this precious baby go up!"

Ekstra, Ian, Sebastian, and Tia moved away from the guard rail and pressed their backs against the wall as the enormous machine moved quietly past them and up through the hole in the roof.

"Wow. That thing is huge. Why do you have such an enormous telescope? Trying to blow up the moon?" Tia joked. She almost had to shout over the alarm. "Don't lasers blow stuff up, like space debris?"

"Ha, ha, yes and no. We are not blowing anything up. A laser is a device that emits light—there are many, many uses for that light. We are sending communications far out into space," Ekstra said, looking up and beyond the telescope to the sky. "It's a lovely evening. Now that the sun has set, the sky should be stunning soon, and crystal clear."

"I thought you said all the solar flare action was blocking communications," Tia said, gazing at the darkening sky. The sun was gone but light still radiated, morphing the sky into a brilliant shade of purple.

"It is, that's why the alarm went off. As soon as we know the flares have blocked communication, we start the laser. That way no one knows what we are doing, not the Department of Defense, Space Force, NASA, nor anyone else doing similar work," Ekstra explained.

"But the flares don't block your work?" Tia asked.

"No, we have very special equipment." Ekstra smiled.

Is that what Nafasi was talking about this morning? Why he was so excited about the collision? Maybe I should have paid more attention.

"We should go down. Ekstra has important work to do, and the time we have available is unpredictable," Sebastian said. "The window could close at any moment."

"That is true. Nafasi thought July 14 was our best opportunity, but I think it's prudent to work as much as possible at every chance. I prefer to leave it up, ready to go, but with the security breach today, we pulled it down. It is a very sensitive piece of equipment. I mean, thanks to the technology Naf obtained, it's more durable than any other telescope in the world, but still, we must take care. Nafasi has advanced free-space optical communication by decades, but time is of the essence, and we are eager to accomplish our goal. I wish he was here," Ekstra said. "Go. I will see you downstairs when this opportunity closes. I will explain more then."

Sebastian led Ian and Tia back to the elevator.

"Are you guys hungry?" Sebastian calmly asked inside the elevator. The alarm was still loud, but not so loud that they had to shout.

"What the hell? Did we just see a huge laser beam?" Ian asked.

"Right? Crazy technology out here in the middle of nowhere. We only saw the laser, not a beam. Can't see the beam with the naked eye. Nafasi was a genius. Or good at collecting geniuses. I mean, he got us all to come out here," Sebastian said with a laid-back smile. "Do you know what laser stands for?"

Tia and Ian shook their heads.

"Light amplification by stimulated emission of radiation. Isn't that cool? I learned it from Ekstra. You can do a million things with lasers," Sebastian said smugly.

"Are we going back to the Center?" Ian asked as they walked out on the ground floor.

Tia looked up at the regular ceiling, wondering what kind of architecture was strong enough to support that enormous machine just a few floors above them.

"Nope, we generally don't mix. The guests and staff support the effort—some financially, some through certain jobs, like medical or tracking—but that is just one part of the operation. The other part is this. Everyone knows what Naf's goals are—were, I guess. But few know the details. Nafasi and Jordisk, even more so, were pretty paranoid that the government would find out and interfere. Or maybe someone like Tia would betray us," Sebastian said. "Come, we have a kitchen and rooms here. Not even remotely as nice as at the Hotel Center, but adequate."

So, they kept Ian in the dark as well. Who are they trying to communicate with in space? Rex? The others?

Do they want more worldwide violence? Do they want to take over the world? They don't trust the United States government even now. Why? Did the government assassinate Nafasi?

"Tia!" Ian snapped, "Earth to Tia?"

"What?" Tia asked. She had been so lost in thought she didn't realize they had entered a kitchen.

"How hungry are you? We have fruit and hummus and some lentil soup we can warm up. I think we have some bread. Is that okay? It's all homemade at the Center," Sebastian said. "We take from the Center but don't cook here. Just warm stuff up."

"That's fine. I usually only eat once a day, but it has been an extraordinary day," Tia said. "Thanks."

"Bummer, the alarm stopped. Power and communications must be back up and running," Sebastian said.

Tia was so tired she barely noticed.

They all sat down at a large metal table in the kitchen. Tia picked at the food. Breakfast seemed so long ago. "What time is it?" Tia asked, yawning.

"About 9 p.m.," Ian replied. "I'm exhausted. You must be dead. We hiked and ran miles, and that was after Jordisk tried to strangle you."

"Fuck! I got distracted by the laser! That violent fuck went after my cat!" Tia cried in alarm, horrified that she had forgotten. "I need to find her."

Clorox could be covered in those burning plastic things!

Tia was rushing out the kitchen door when she heard Sebastian loudly speak into a radio. She turned back to listen.

"Hello, Mr. Jordisk. This is Sebastian. We are about to put the prisoner—I mean, Tia—to bed. Have you located the cat?" Sebastian asked.

"No, I had to return to the Hotel Center. I need you and Ian to find it and bring it to me," Jordisk replied.

"It's dark now. How about we look in the morning? I doubt it will put much distance between itself and Tia," Ian said.

"Okay, fine. But I want it first thing in the morning," Jordisk said before the radio went dead.

Ian looked at Tia with raised eyebrows and out-stretched hands, seemingly pleased they'd solved the problem.

"Well, that sucks," Sebastian said.

"Why? Do you think he is lying? That he has Clorox?" Tia asked.

"What? No. Jordisk has more important things to do. He would want us to look for it. It sucks that the radio is working, which means no sunspots and no laser. That window was short. Ekstra should be down soon. Hopefully, the alarm goes off again," Sebastian said. "We got these old primitive radios hoping the flares would not affect them, but they go out like everything else."

Well, Sebastian sure has bought into this crazy bullshit. Seems like Ian has as well. I need to get out of here. I don't want any more lectures from the mad scientist tonight.

"Sebastian, if you knew he would not look, why did you try and send that serial assaulter after my cat?' Tia asked.

"It was just a distraction. When Mr. Jordisk is about to blow, it's better to distract him. Once he calms down, he's fine. It worked." Sebastian shrugged. "I've seen Nafasi calm him down before. I mean, it's great he takes all this so seriously, but sometimes he goes over the top."

"I'm tired. I'm going to sleep. I don't mind sleeping outside. I'll find Clorox, no worries," Tia said, heading toward the door again.

"Not so fast. I will show you to your room. Jordisk would kill us if we lost you. No distraction is big enough to handle that! He thinks you killed Nafasi, so, no, you are not sleeping outside," Sebastian said. "Please follow me."

"Why does he think I killed Nafasi? Just because of the day I arrived?" Tia asked.

"No, he's convinced he saw you snooping around the property before. He claims he has been tracking you for weeks," Sebastian replied.

Twenty-Six

Sebastian led Tia down the hall. He held a door open, and Tia stuck her head in before entering the small room with a single bed, a small dresser, and a half bathroom.

A glorified jail cell?

"Bet you wish you stayed in the hotel now. Some of those rooms are fantastic. Everything is fancy there—even the staff quarters are nice," Sebastian said.

"It's fine," Tia said, tossing her backpack on the floor and kicking the door shut in Sebastian's face.

She flopped down on the bed, feeling guilty about the kick until she heard the click.

That fucker locked me in!

Tia snapped awake from a nightmare that her foster dad Rick was an alien. He explained that she was also from outer space and that he was going to eat her. He wanted to wrap her up in a bean burrito and have her for dinner. He explained that was the main reason he encouraged her to work at Taco Bell and become a manager—not for her to learn practical life skills, but so he could eat her in a burrito.

This place and these people are making me crazy.

Tia jumped when the alarm went off. It was not as sharp as when she was out near the source, but it was loud enough to be annoying. She felt strong and healed and realized her senses were keen again. Yesterday, she had been weaker than she realized. The shock, long hike, and being choked had taken a toll on her body and mind.

Once the alarm stopped, she tried to go back to sleep. After a while, she tried the door, but it was locked. She knocked.

"Ian? Sebastian? Are you out there? Let me out. I feel claustrophobic in here," Tia said to the closed door.

The lock clicked and the door flew open.

"Well, I'm sick of sitting out here. Happy you're up. Let's go," Ian said.

Ian led her to the kitchen where Sebastian and Ekstra were having coffee. "Good morning, Tia," Ekstra said, seeming pleased to see her.

"I heard the alarm earlier, thought you would be with your laser," Tia replied.

"We had to bring it back in already," Ekstra answered. "That window was very short. They must get longer. We need more time. Let's hope Nafasi was right about the 14th."

"It's going to work, Ekstra. It must," Sebastian said.

"Why 'must' it work? What exactly are you trying to do?" Tia asked.

Just act interested in their ridiculous story, gain some trust, and then ask to go for a walk to find Clorox.

"Ian said you grew up like most of us. That you can't remember your parents or any relatives. You bumped around foster homes all your life. That is common for those of us that look strange. Well, even when we look normal, there is always something off. Where did we come from? Where were we found? A few, despite our looks and strange origin, do end up with good families and, sometimes, wealthy ones. Me, Nafasi, and some of the other guests were adopted by families that invested in us. That is how Nafasi could afford all this. He had wealthy parents. His father died in a helicopter crash a few years before the shooting and his brother and mother both shot themselves. Nafasi inherited billions, enabling him to pursue his quest for answers." Ekstra took a long sip of coffee as tears filled his eyes. "I can't believe he is gone."

Tia looked away, uncomfortable with emotional pain. She located a mug and poured a cup of coffee, even though she never cared for it.

Impatient to find Clorox, she broke the sad, awkward silence with a question.

"So, you all think you are extraterrestrials, like Rex, and from outer space?" Tia asked.

"No, not necessarily like Rex. But yes, extraterrestrials from outer space," Ian replied.

"Why? Why would you think something so ludicrous?" Tia asked.

She knew it was what they believed but saying it out loud, so calmly and matter-of-factly, almost made Tia laugh. She refrained only because Ekstra still looked upset.

"Nafasi figured it out when he was young. He knew he was different; he had the confidence to not just think he was weird or a freak." Ekstra sighed. "He recognized he was special. He said his adoptive parents were loving and supportive and wondered about his peculiarities. They had him checked by doctors and therapists and when his peculiarities weren't considered dangerous, they accepted them and moved on. That gave him space to wonder and research. He traveled the world and talked to leading scientists in many fields."

"He did tell me that yesterday," Tia interjected. She did not want another space language lecture.

"He spoke to astronauts and astrophysicists and chased down strange people and strange leads. Most of us had different experiences. I doubt your foster families acknowledged your differences; much less made you feel comfortable with them. Nafasi, like most of us, ate very little. His parents and teachers would notice. Most foster parents don't care. We are all stronger than humans. While none that I know have Superman's power, everyone has some extraordinary abilities," Ekstra said.

"I think Mr. Jordisk would be the closest to Superman. He has amazing skills," Sebastian added.

Tia nodded to encourage Ekstra to keep speaking. She was interested in their origin and family stories, even if she thought he was deranged.

Aliens? Really?

"Nafasi was good at seeing us. He said we look like humans, but more intense. We're blonder or more brunette. Our eyes are very distinctive in different ways. We have energy swirling off our bodies—just everything about us is more vivid," Ekstra continued.

"Like those old *Men In Black* movies? Once he could spot them, did he see aliens everywhere?" Tia swallowed her laughter.

"You don't see it, Tia?" Ekstra asked softly.

"What about her cat?" Ian asked. "Maybe it's from space?"

"Maybe, or it's just a clever cat," Ekstra said with a smile. "I have heard of others with animals, I think, though I have never seen it. We seem to take common forms. We look human. I guess we could be any animal. We don't look like E.T., a giant orange tabby, or anything from a horror movie. Well, not yet anyway," Ekstra explained.

"What do you think, Tia?" Ian asked gently.

Tia just shrugged. But her mind exploded with possibilities.

Where did Clorox come from? She showed up in the Taco Bell parking lot, full-grown and healthy, and followed me home. The cat never entered the house or restaurant; she was just always there, outside, waiting for me. At first, I worried she would get hit by a car or in a fight with another animal, but it has been seven years now since we met and the cat has never needed my help until Tom Jordisk attacked her. Or did Clorox attack Tom?

"Everyone here, at the Center, is an alien?" Tia asked.

"No, not everyone. Some of the staff are regular people, but most are like us. The humans know this is an unusual place with unusual people. We trust our staff," Sebastian cut in.

"Ekstra, how did you meet Nafasi?" Tia asked.

"I came to America from the West Indies to study engineering at Carnegie Mellon, with a focus on aerospace. I met Nafasi at a lecture on campus about the possibility of life on other planets, focusing on single cells and other primitive species. It was based on the Earth-focused assumption that species on other planets would evolve as humans did here. I heard Naf make some snarky comments under his breath about the lack of imagination and the speaker's education. When it was over, I followed him out to ask him about his comments. He said he was delighted to meet me and that he had noticed me before, that he was attracted to my vibrant energy and eyes. I just thought he was hitting on me, which he was," Ekstra said, smiling as he told the story. "He said there had to be sophisticated life on other planets, not just things crawling out of cosmic muck. He said we were aliens from another planet. It took several dates before I believed him. That was in 2014. Six years later, with the arrival of Rex, he would be proven correct."

Sebastian, Ian, and Ekstra watched Tia's face.

"Now you have had the talk. Nafasi should have told you that he discovered the truth. He is great at telling the story. Was great, I guess," Ekstra said sadly.

"You must believe us now, Tia," Ian added.

The alarm suddenly went off, startling everyone. Ekstra and Sebastian jumped up, rushing to the door.

"Stay focused! Today is July 13. We only have until tomorrow to fulfill Nafasi's dream," Ekstra said before walking out the door.

Twenty-Seven

Tia sat at the table thinking.

Their story kind of makes sense. Of course extraterrestrials, like Rex and the others, could live here among us. Rex was all-powerful. If the rest are like him, they can do anything. But they lost me when they said I'm an extraterrestrial too. That is just fucking ridiculous.

"How does—*did*—Nafasi identify aliens? Just from the hair, eyes, and quirky mannerisms?" Tia asked Ian. "He sends you out to find a woman with strange hair and missing irises and you track me down in Deep Creek, Maryland?"

"Nope, it's more complicated than that. Nafasi studied himself, his own body, and worked with the greatest universities and minds in the world. He figured out that his body is six percent nitrogen. Nitrogen comprises only three percent of the human body by mass. It's found in all organisms in amino acids and nucleic acids, DNA and RNA, and adenosine triphosphate, which is an essential energy transfer molecule. That is what I got from hearing Naf give 'the talk' to newbies. Nafasi created a gadget that can detect people with high levels of nitrogen in their bodies. He pays people all over the world to use his machines.

When they come across someone with high nitrogen, they contact him and we start tracking."

"The people he pays, are they human or extraterrestrial?" Tia asked.

"Both, mostly human. He tells them he needs to find people with high nitrogen to be potential organ donors. People tend to want to help, especially post-Pledge. And he pays them," Ian replied.

"Why the extra nitrogen?" Tia asked.

"Don't know. Nafasi didn't either. He just found it to be a common characteristic of our kind and a trait that is dramatically different from humans."

"Do you have one of those gadgets that can sense excess nitrogen?"

"No, I don't need one. I can tell a person is not human by the time I get near them. The tracking part can take some time. I get a general location, picture, and some details, like where they might work. Sometimes, I do online research and search their history and socials, I watch them for days, and when I'm 100 percent sure, I move in," Ian said with a casual shrug.

"Does anyone here have one?" Tia asked, her heart beating fast.

No way I'm an alien. Not me. I'll prove it to them by waving the wand or whatever on myself.

"I would like to see the gadget," she added.

"I'm sure Ekstra has one. He has a lot of tech here. Why? Do you need proof? Still don't believe us?" Ian asked.

"Nope, I still don't believe it entirely. I want to test Clorox too," Tia said. "Let's go find her."

Twenty-Eight

Tia walked out of the strange building and into the early morning light. She moved quickly past the manicured grass surrounding the building to the tree line. She slowly walked the perimeter, watching for any sudden movement.

"Can't you call her?" Ian whispered in her ear, making Tia jump.

"What the hell, Ian! Don't sneak up on me like that!" Tia whispered back.

"I've been right behind you since you walked through the door. See, I'm a damn good tracker!" Ian responded quietly. "The insects are super loud out here, all their munching and moving is a distraction. And the birds are waking up."

"Shush, be quiet," Tia whispered, putting more space between her and Ian. "Before I came here, I used to think I had a keen hearing. But now, I don't think so."

"Because you were comparing yourself to humans," Ian replied.

Tia strained her ears to hear any rustling sounds. After a lap around the forest's edge, she went several feet in and started the loop again. She inhaled deeply, enjoying the smell of wild berries, acorns, and hickory nuts. She could hear the singing of warblers and other songbirds as they flew about. One particularly loud woodpecker was very busy. The air was still. Tia knew it would be another hot day.

It's strange that it's taking this long to find her. Maybe Ian and Sebastian lied and Jordisk catnapped her?

Tia jumped when Ian tapped her shoulder. He had been so quiet, that she forgot he was there. She turned to tell him to fuck off, but he was pointing off in the distance with a grin on his face.

Clorox?

Tia scanned the forest for the cat but gasped when she spotted a black bear several hundred feet away. It sat on a downed tree trunk, breaking off pieces of bark. Suddenly, it stood on its back legs and violently shook the trunk, oblivious to their presence, or maybe he just didn't care. Tia smiled and had to stop herself from laughing in pure joy. Seeing healthy animals living a natural life in their environment always made her happy. Tia and Ian watched for several minutes before the delightful animal wandered off, in search of more dead trees full of tasty insects.

"So cool," Ian said as it disappeared into the forest.

"See, being quiet serves many purposes," Tia whispered as she started walking again, looking around for the cat.

A loud commotion from the direction of the building caused them to jump. Tia squatted down, pulling Ian with her. Angry voices penetrated the forest, but they were too far to make out the words. She could also hear something metal slamming against metal.

Tia crept closer to the edge of the forest, slinking behind bushes and trees. When she got close enough to see across the lawn, she gasped.

It was the same group of men that had spooked Nafasi when they drove into town.

The same men who spoke to him on the porch before she met him for breakfast.

A few wore business suits and others were dressed in identical black uniforms reminiscent of a SWAT team. There were more than had been at the Center yesterday. From afar, yesterday's interaction had seemed congenial, but today appeared tense.

Jordisk and the two older gentlemen with the perfectly coiffed beards walked around from the far side of the building. Tia strained her ears to hear what was being said but to no avail. The loud woodpecker was close and banging its head nonstop.

"Dammit, I can't hear, can you?" Tia whispered to Ian. "Who are they?"

"Maybe Space Force? Or the Department of Defense? CIA?" Ian guessed quietly.

"Some look like city SWAT cops from before the shooting," Tia whispered, glancing over her shoulder at him.

"Maybe we should hide? Go deeper in the woods or back to the Hotel Center?" Ian asked. "This does not look good."

"Or maybe you should come with us and join the conversation?" A woman said from behind a black helmet with a full-face guard. She'd come from deeper in the woods with two others, all dressed in the same menacing uniform.

"Holy shit! Are those guns?" Tia said as three AR-15 rifles were pointed at her. Tia started to shake with pure primal fear. She had never owned or touched a gun before the shooting and certainly hadn't since. But she recognized these terrifying weapons of mass destruction.

Memories rushed through her mind. The woman in the car in the drive-thru at Taco Bell with a bullet hole between her eyes. Children crying in their front yards, pleading with her to come inside and help their mom or dad. The smell of rust and human waste. The wailing that poured from apartments and houses. A few people stumbling around, covered in blood.

The walk home from work, when she finally had the confidence to leave the restaurant, was the scariest twenty minutes of her life. People were screaming and running. Some ran from dead bodies and guns; some ran in search of help. *Call 911! Call 911! What's happening? Where are the police?* Terrified, Tia just kept walking, frantically looking over her shoulders, ready to run if someone or something came at her.

She snapped back to reality as the gunmen moved closer.

"Point those fucking things somewhere else," Tia snarled.

Twenty-Nine

They stood in silence, staring at one other.

"I said, point those fucking guns elsewhere. In fact, get the fuck out of my presence, out of this forest, and out of this world you psycho, violent creeps!" Tia shouted.

"Okay, fine. Lower your weapons," the woman said from behind her mask. The others immediately obeyed. "Come with us."

The three SWAT people slowly slung their weapons over their shoulders.

"Ian, do you feel like returning to the building?" Tia asked.

"Maybe? I sure as hell would like to know who these trespassing, armed assholes are. This is private property, for fuck's sake," Ian replied.

Tia felt emboldened by his confidence. They would only return to the building because it was their choice, not because some weapons were pointed at them. She locked eyes with him.

"And I want to be sure everyone is okay. So yes, I do want to return to the building. Thank you for asking Tia." Ian shook his head in disgust. "Ready?"

"Yes, let's go," Tia said, turning toward the building.

"Why were you hiding in the woods?" the woman asked.

"Hiding? We were talking and walking in nature. It's fantastic out here. But then we were frightened by hostile strangers with guns. We live and adhere to The Pledge. I have no idea who you are or what you are doing. Looks to me like you're trying to bring violence back," Tia replied sharply, knowing that people with guns always seem to feel the need to kill.

It's like the machine creeps into their mind and soul. Gun owners seem happy to kill an animal and claim it's hunting. And what is hunting anyway? Go a few years as a vegan and hunting just becomes violent murder.

As they approached the building, they saw Jordisk and the others arguing.

"There is no way in hell you're entering this building. You may return with us to the Hotel Center, and we can have a discussion. None of you are entering this private business on private property," Jordisk said, his face filled with calm fury. It was nothing like the rage he'd displayed in the ballroom after Nafasi's murder.

He's treating these armed assholes better than he treated me. Must be the guns.

"How did everyone get up here? Will you walk back to the Hotel Center? That is a several-hour hike. I sure hope you don't trip and shoot yourselves," Tia said snarkily, to no one in particular. She was angry with all of them.

"There is a service road not far from here. I assume they drove up and snuck through the woods. Were you coming to kill us? Was that your plan?" Jordisk asked a man in a business suit. He nodded at the three SWAT cops with the AR-15 rifles. "Those are nasty machines. One tiny bullet, and one tiny hole, can melt multiple organs. From here or 1000 feet away, you could paralyze or kill us all in less than twenty seconds. You must feel very powerful—like Gods."

"We're not here to kill anyone. We're taking precautions. After all, you're firing an extremely powerful laser beam into space. And we demand to know why," a man in a suit replied.

"Who are you?" Tia asked impertinently.

Fuck all these people. I'm not on anyone's side. Not the so-called extraterrestrials that have tried to kill me nor the assholes with guns.

"I'm General Carlos White with Space Force. These men are with me," he said nodding his head toward two other men in suits. "These are officials with the Department of Defense. The others are soldiers."

"If you're all military, why aren't you in uniforms like your soldiers?" Ian asked. "Hiding what you are?"

"No, of course not, son. Since the mass shooting, few people wear uniforms. They have been considered relics of our violent past, used to intimidate people," General White replied.

"So why are these scary, faceless soldiers wearing uniforms? I mean, just the guns are enough to scare the shit out of any thinking or feeling person," Tia said, hoping she was pissing everyone off with her questions. "Why are they here? Why are all of you here?"

"Young lady, our conversation is not with you. We demand access to inspect this building. We also need to speak to Nafasi Genny. We assume he is here since he was not at the Hotel Center. We spoke to Mr. Genny yesterday; he will not be surprised that we have returned," General White replied.

Tia looked at Ian who was looking at Jordisk. No one even flinched.

"Okay, let's go find Nafasi. Only he can let you in. He's not here. I think he's back at the Hotel Center," Jordisk said. "Ian and Tia, stay here. That's an order." He and his silent security colleagues started to walk toward the forest.

"Sure thing, Mr. Jordisk," Ian replied.

"Should we stay here?" the masked woman in SWAT gear asked General White. "Guard the telescope?"

"No, come along. We need to speak to Mr. Genny," General White said over his shoulder as he followed Jordisk. He paused, turning back to look at the woman, "I mean, they can't move the equipment quickly—it's huge. And our satellites will track what they are doing anyway. Soon, we will return, investigate, and have an open and honest conversation about what is hap- pening here."

"Okay, boss," the woman said, marching with the group toward the tree line. Just before she stepped into the shade of the woods, she took off her helmet, revealing straight black hair that blended into the blackness of her uniform, gun, and helmet.

The woman glanced over her shoulder at Tia.

They locked eyes.

She had black, iris-less eyes.

Just like Tia's.

Thirty

Tia gasped. She had never seen eyes so like hers. She stared for several seconds after the woman disappeared into the forest, heading to the service road Tia had only just learned existed.

Who is she? What is she? They keep telling me I am from outer space, maybe she is as well? She has a huge gun and radiates violence. She is nothing like me.

Except for those eyes.

"It's weird that there is a service road somewhere nearby. Makes it feel less wild. I kind of hate roads. It would be more fun to hike through the woods and back to the Center. Should we look for your cat? Oh shit, we need to warn Ekstra. He may not know what is up, depending on the power and communication situation. Tia, are you okay, Tia?" Ian asked. "Earth to Tia."

"Yes, fine. Ian, did you notice anything strange about that woman?" Tia asked, still looking at the woods.

She can't be one of them, or us, or whatever. Ian said he could just tell. Or was that only after he had done research? I'm sure the others can tell, right? Or do they all need the nitrogen detector machine? Does Jordisk know?

The heavy main doors opened, slamming against the exterior walls.

They both jumped.

"Come in now, before they return!" Ekstra said in his thick Caribbean accent. "Quickly!"

Ian and Tia followed Ekstra in and watched as he slammed and locked the doors.

"I saw them on camera walking up the hill toward us before everything went down but did not hear them speak. Damn! We have missed a long window. At least fifteen minutes! We had to turn off the alarm and could not engage the laser until we knew they'd left. Dammit, those government idiots might cause more delays!" Ekstra said, clearly upset by the situation.

"They said they know you're shooting a laser into space using a powerful telescope, so I guess, you don't have to stop now. Since you're not using it because they're here, they are already causing delays," Ian explained.

"Okay. Come," Ekstra led them to the elevator, impatiently pressing the up button. "Good to know, Ian. We will not delay any longer for them."

"Is there a basement?" Tia asked, noticing a down button option.

"Yes, yes, there is," Ekstra said as the elevator doors opened for them. "But that does not matter. What else did they say?"

"They said they are from Space Force and the Department of Defense and the regular army too. They had guns, Ekstra! Can you fucking believe it? Could you see that on the cameras? They pointed AR-15 assault weapons—or rifles, or whatever they are called—at me and Tia while we were walking in the woods! So, now, what, our government has zero respect for The Pledge? For the seventy million Americans that lost their lives in the shooting? I'm appalled by the callous arrogance! It's nuts!" Ian replied.

"What do they want?" Ekstra asked.

"To know what we're doing here, in this building. They know about the laser. They want to see it," Ian explained.

"Where are they now?" Ekstra asked.

"Jordisk was pretty calm. Convinced them to go back to the Hotel Center. They want to speak to Nafasi."

Ekstra raised his eyebrows.

"Jordisk escorted them back to find him. Pretty strange that the psychopath was so calm with outsiders armed with at least three big guns, but chose to almost choke me to death, an innocent unarmed person, over something I didn't do," Tia said angrily.

"We need to calm down and focus," Ekstra said as the elevator door opened. "Come, let's go to the lab and make sure everything is ready. Who knows what may happen next? We don't have Naf and his charm to deal with the government anymore."

"But they don't know that yet," Ian reminded him.

Tia followed Ian and Ekstra through a door that was strangely round to accommodate the round building. She had not paid attention to the floor they got out on but since the hole in the ceiling seemed higher, she knew she was on a lower floor than she had been on yesterday. Upon entering the room, she noticed Sebastian, who was working on a computer. They made brief eye contact and he nodded. There were two others in the room, who were also looking at computers. She thought she recognized them from the party, but they were dressed so differently, it was hard to tell.

Ian fist-bumped Sebastian and filled him in on what had happened. He told him about the guns. He kept referring to the general, his colleagues, and staff as "humans."

Tia walked around the small, cramped room and looked at the different machines and computers. She had no idea what they were doing or what they were for, and she did not care. She could not get the eyes of the intimidating woman dressed in full SWAT gear out of her mind.

Come on Tia, are you actually starting to believe their bullshit? Maybe she has aniridia.

"Ekstra," Tia said loudly, to be heard above the men's chatter. "What exactly does the laser do? Does it blow up debris to make things safe for 'the others'? Are you trying to help the extraterrestrials, like Kate and Sinclair did?"

All eyes snapped to Tia.

"No, no, Tia, that is *not* what we're doing," Ekstra replied.

"So? What is it?"

Ian and Ekstra exchanged a glance.

"We are calling to the others," Ekstra said.

"The others?" Tia gasped.

"Yes, well, to any extraterrestrial who can come to Earth—or come *back* to Earth—and take us with them. We don't know why they left us here, or how we came to be here, but after Rex and July 14 and the cloud, we know our kind is out there. We want to go home," Ekstra said softly.

"Wait, you're calling Rex and the others to come back? After they caused a global blood bath and killed hundreds of millions of people? Seriously? What the hell!?" Tia snapped in shock.

Thirty-One

"Tia, the humans shot themselves, remember?" Ekstra said.

"Because Rex brainwashed them into doing it, remember?!" Tia responded.

"Tia, we aren't asking for more violence. We just want to go home. We wish everyone would just leave us be to do our work. We are not violent. We did not bring guns anywhere—the humans did. They came here and threatened us, why are you concerned about them? Their nature is violent and hateful. We just want to leave," Ekstra said, sounding more emotional and less gentle.

Tia walked around the room, thinking. Everyone was watching her. "Where did you get this equipment, the super powerful telescope and laser?" Tia asked.

"Nafasi was working for NASA when the collision happened. The collision that killed Rex's people. Naf tracked the debris, helped collect it, and moved it to Kennedy Space Center for storage and research. He determined right away that many of the materials were not of Earth. He kept some, stole some, and bought some. He said they didn't belong to NASA or the American space industry. Hell, many, *many* nations have advanced space programs; it was arrogant of

America to cover it up, to try and keep it for themselves," Ekstra explained.

"Huh, that sounds like a violation of The Pledge, which he claimed to adhere to," Tia responded.

"But The Pledge came later, Tia," Ekstra said with a loud, exasperated sigh. "Naf was suspicious that we were extraterrestrials before the deadly collision, it just provided proof. Naf discovered the increased nitrogen levels in himself, other organics, and the materials from space before July 14 and was refining the hypothesis that it was evidence of extraterrestrials and extraterrestrial activity. The mass shooting just confirmed his hypothesis. Nafasi is brilliant. Or *was* brilliant," Ekstra said. "And he brought us all together to share this knowledge, and taught us how to use it to try and go home."

"It's cool, Tia," Sebastian said. "And Naf worked with Sinclair and Kate after they cleared the space debris. Naf figured out they—Kate, Sinclair, and Rex—were working together. Humans and extraterrestrials worked together to clean up space."

"They worked together to stop *more* global violence—maybe the annihilation of the planet! It's not some cool sci-fi movie plot. Rex killed hundreds of millions of people! They worked together to stop 'the others' from killing more!" Tia was practically shouting. "Do you think the mass killing was a good thing?"

"No, of course not, Tia. We all lost people on July 14," Ian replied. "The world changed forever. But, come on, you must admit that the world is better now. The Pledge has made people kinder and taught them to think rationally about their consumption and the abuse of nature, the planet, and each other. Global warming gases are declining so fast. When was the last time you saw garbage on the ground or used a plastic straw, bag, or fruit container? Wildlife is recovering quickly everywhere. The oceans are full of fish, dolphins, and whales. People—the government, corporations, and the media—all said it couldn't be done. They were ready to just give up—let nature and humankind die. Drown the world, and space, in pollution. But look what the mass shooting did: it made us change, save ourselves."

"But seventy million Americans died! That day was horrific, tragic, and violent!" Tia said, putting her hands over her face in frustration.

He is right; things are much better now. But bringing back the others? To do what?

"Yes, well, let's talk about the violence for a moment. America was hit the hardest and suffered the most. America had double the rate of civilian gun ownership to the second-place country, the Falkland Islands, did you know that? My island, and many in the Caribbean, had gun problems but they were incomparable to America's. The other big gun nations were hit hard—Serbia, Montenegro, Yemen, Uruguay, Canada, and Finland—but still nothing in comparison to America. Even nations with huge armed military and police forces were unparalleled because America has a huge army and the most police forces. So yes, the shooting was a tragedy worldwide, but mostly for America. We all live here. Many of Nafasi's staff and guests are from other countries, but we chose to be here because America is awesome. I guess I'm trying to put it in perspective. Other nations had fewer guns, and thus, fewer deaths that day, but were suffering more from global warming, pollution, and geopolitical crisis. Live by the gun, die by the gun," Ekstra said with a dramatic shrug.

It's true. The mass shooting was worse here. America caused most of the pollution, with its disease of mass consumption, and its encouraged collective cognitive dissonance about so many things. All the greed, depression, and mistrust were putting the nation on the fast track to fascism or a civil war. Everyone hated everyone until the mass shooting brought us together, but I'm not going to give them the satisfaction of admitting it.

"And from the look of the guns pointed at us today, I think America might be heading backward," Ian added.

"Okay, but what about Jordisk? He attacked me in town and tried to strangle me in the safe room after Nafasi was shot! You know I didn't shoot him! Yet, everyone seems okay with me being almost killed!" Tia shouted.

Sebastian cleared his throat. "He heard that one of us was working with the government; he wasn't taking any chances. For some reason, he felt very strongly that it was you."

Thirty-Two

"**N**o way. You know it wasn't me," Tia replied, clenching her fists in frustration.

Maybe it's that woman with the gun?

She could be an extraterrestrial working with the government. Maybe she does not know what she is? But if I assume she is from space, just because I saw her eyes, is that presumptuous? Ableist? She could have aniridia.

An alarm blared.

Tia jumped.

"Lower that volume, now!" Ekstra shouted.

"Okay, lowering volume. The army, Jordisk, and his security team drove far enough away, I lost them on our cameras before we lost all communications. They will have no idea what is going on up here. Since they didn't hear the alarm, we are good to go," said one of the techies staring at the computer screens.

"Fire when ready, my friend." Ekstra rubbed his palms together them pressed them into a prayer position. "Let's hope this is the one!"

Tia walked over to a desk chair and sat down, casually spinning it on its wheels.

I'm not sure I want this to be 'the one.' Everyone here seems a bit too casual about the prospect of more violence. We got lucky that, before, it was just humans that were killed, that wildlife and their ecosystems didn't suffer because of our selfish behavior. I mean, in most sci-fi stories, the catastrophic event wipes out nature, leaving starving people to become cannibalistic on their path to dystopia, like in The Road. Then there's Skynet, rogue mushrooms, or zombies; hell, if they had not found a vaccine for the coronavirus so soon after the shooting, everyone and everything might be dead now. Animals caught COVID too.

"I'm thirsty. I'm going to the kitchen," Ian said. "Want to come?"

"What?" Tia asked, the question pulling her out of her musings.

"Let's go to the kitchen. I'm thirsty. We are not helping here anyway," Ian said.

He moved to hold open the door for Tia.

"Okay, I'll go. But I don't need a guard," Tia snapped, still unsettled by all the new information.

"No, but you could get lost. I'm an excellent tracker. I can always find a kitchen," Ian replied.

Tia almost laughed. Ever since the first time she spoke to him, she liked the way he talked.

"Huh, but can you always tell if a person isn't human? In the woods, you said you could tell, right? You know what percent of nitrogen they are without the device?" Tia asked.

They were waiting for the elevator. The door opened and they got in.

"I don't know what percentage of nitrogen they are. By the time I get close, I just know. Whether it is instinctive or just from practice, I'm not sure. For example, when I was tracking you, Naf said someone in a restaurant in Georgia saw you. You were a waitress and had strange eyes and a vibrant look. That person reached out to whoever had the device nearby. And by 'nearby,' I mean in the tri-state area. That person followed up and zapped you, confirming you had high levels of nitrogen. That's when I was called in. I went to the restaurant, but you had moved on. I spoke to people at and near the restaurant, found out where you were staying, and determined which day you left town. I figured out your general direction through the people you hitchhiked with and caught up with you in Maryland. I had a photo of you from the beginning. Your eyes are an easy way to track you; people remember them. Plus, your unusual mannerisms," Ian explained as the doors opened on the ground floor.

"Were you following me in Deep Creek?" Tia asked, weirded out. She had been stalked and had no idea!

"Yes, I just asked around and showed people your picture. They said they saw you on a trail. I followed you for a few days, all the way to your amazing mansion. When I thought it was the right time, I broke in and waited for you on the deck," Ian said. "Here's the kitchen!"

"You sound surprised," Tia replied, as she headed to the refrigerator.

"All the doors look alike. I was worried I wouldn't open the right door and you would lose faith in my tracking skills," Ian said, smiling.

Tia almost laughed. *He really is agreeable ... for a stalker.*

"You know that stalking people is creepy, right? And you lied to me. There were like fifty people here when I arrived, plus a psychopath that wanted to kill me," Tia responded.

"I didn't know!" Ian exclaimed. "Everyone usually leaves the Center in early July. They head out to other places with lasers and technology. I never went with them. I just assumed they were doing the same thing: conducting research or partying somewhere more exotic. I heard they were in Hawaii last year. For a couple of summers, they were doing construction and renovations. This is the first July they spent here since I started working for Naf. I didn't lie; I just didn't know."

"Whatever," Tia said, filling a glass with water and taking a huge swig.

"And I did not lie, nor was I mistaken, about anything else. All I said was that the Hill View Hotel was surrounded by natural beauty and amazing gardens, had a spectacular view, and no one was there, and you were hooked. I got rid of your easily traced cell phone and left after you fell asleep. Easy. You made all the decisions on your own," Ian said, filling a water bottle.

"Why does that piss me off?" Tia asked. "Like I'm some dumbass that is easily conned. I will say if you had called it the Hill View Hotel Center, that would have been a red flag. I would never go to a Center."

"Ha, no way! You are as independent and streetsmart as they come. It's the Hill View Hotel Center but some people still call it a hotel, some call it the Center, or both. Still not a lie. And we are both foster kids and from another planet. I think we both sensed that bond and so we immediately trusted each other. That happens to a lot of us here," Ian replied.

Tia felt her face getting hot.

That made sense. But also, Ian is sweet and handsome and loves nature as much as I do. Ian is the only person I like and trust here.

"I've heard you refer to them as 'humans' a couple of times. You're starting to accept what you are, right? With those amazing eyes that see only beauty. Are you starting to accept how special you are?" Ian asked.

Tia furrowed her brows.

Is he hitting on me? Or using his mad tracker skills to manipulate me again? I will test him.

"Well, okay then. The laser seems to be working. The nutbag led the gun-toting goons away. There is nothing left for me to see here. I think I will find Clorox and hit the road," Tia said. "It was interesting meeting you and finding this place. You have given me a lot to think about."

"I'm coming with you. You can't go out there alone. Jordisk might still want to kill you. Hell, he may have already killed the government people if they pissed him off enough," Ian said.

"What the fuck!" Tia exclaimed. "Are you serious?"

Thirty-Three

"Come on, let's look for your cat. It will be nice to get out of here," Ian said, as he walked over and held the kitchen door open.

"How can you so casually suggest murder? What about The Pledge? What is Jordisk?" Tia asked as they walked to the main door.

"There are different kinds of us. Are we all from different planets? Are there just different kinds of us living on the same planet? I kind of like that image, like the bar scene in Star Wars. Some of us are angry we were left here. Is Earth the foster planet of the galaxy? Was it an experiment? Did something terrible happen to our planet or planets? There are so many unanswered questions. Personally, I kind of like it here so I'm not angry, just curious about what I am and where I'm from. I would love to go and see it. Some feel like they are trapped here, and resent being here, on Earth," Ian explained as they walked.

"Wowza, I hadn't thought of any of that," Tia said, walking into the woods. Her nose was delighted by the powerful scent of pine trees. She scanned the forest floor for Clorox.

"Some of us are more angry and violent. Jordisk probably thought he was protecting us when he attacked you. I think he convinced himself you set up the shooting of Nafasi, even though you were right next to him. I don't know. But clearly, he was wrong about you. Maybe he was wrong about his whole government spy infiltrator theory too," Ian said, with a shrug. "Why do you call your cat Clorox?"

"'Cause she looks like a calico that was dipped in bleach," Tia responded.

"Ha, like humans look compared to us! I love it!" Ian said, clapping his hands enthusiastically.

"Obviously I had not thought of that when I named her," Tia said with a furrowed brow.

"Clorox!" Ian called into the woods. "Here kitty, kitty, kitty!"

"Were Nafasi and Ekstra in a relationship?" Tia asked. "Ekstra occasionally said things that made me think they were."

"They did. They were together for a long time, years. I'm not sure what the situation is now, or was, I guess. This is a 'free love, no judgment' Center. Remember those pre-Pledge posters, that read, 'no homophobia, no racism, no sexism, no hate, no speciesism, no ableism, we accept all mixed couples, including mixed species from different planets?'"

"No, I don't remember those posters! Something similar but not quite so inclusive," Tia said, laughing. "It is funny how you don't see those posters or yard signs around anymore. It's like the stupid hate-based culture wars went the way of guns—gone! And The Pledge helped clarify that love and kindness rule."

"Yes, there have been good changes. So, Naf and Ekstra may or may not have been lovers recently, but they were best friends. It's like they thought as one when it came to the original hypothesis, extensive research, Center structure, and how everything is implemented," Ian replied.

"What about the others? Are they coupled up?" Tia asked.

"Some, I guess. The ones I have brought here seem rather reserved and don't discuss personal stuff with me. I know I was ecstatic to meet others like me. I grew up thinking I was a strange kid. Being parentless already made me strange. But I was always stronger than the other kids. Not enormously so, but just strong enough for kids to notice and point it out. So, I learned to hide it. Just like having better vision, and an extraordinary sense of smell. Well, that was a problem. At one foster home, I kept asking that they take out the garbage because it smelled terrible. Turned out, it was not just the trash, the house stunk, and it really bothered me. I spent months sitting in the yard, smelling grass, weeds, soil, anything to clear my nose. They thought I was strange and were eager to get rid of me. At another house, we lived near a refinery. It was horrible. The smell of oil and chemicals gave me chronic headaches. I vomited constantly. I even smelled it at school. A teacher called me 'chemo sensitive,' which just became a reason for the kids, and my foster family, to make fun of me. They said I was weak and would have to get used to it. It broke my heart that dolphins, whales, sea turtles, fish, birds, and everything else had to smell that unnatural chemical stink all the time. I never got used to it. I just ran away and ended up with another family. When

I turned seventeen, I left the system and moved to New Orleans, which can smell terrible sometimes, but it didn't give me raging headaches. Plus, strange is normal in New Orleans. No one seemed to notice or care about my quirks," Ian explained.

He glanced at Tia and she nodded her head, encouraging him to continue.

I had similar experiences while growing up. Nice to know I was not alone.

"And humans! Wow, did they smell! Detergents, shampoo, moisturizers, hair dye, deodorant, perfume, make-up, medicine, soap, dry cleaning, so many chemicals—it could be overwhelming. Most of it used just to cover bacteria, which does not smell bad if one is clean. Of course, since the shooting people have used fewer chemicals so they can adhere to The Pledge. Another good change," Ian continued. "We have almost no odor, nothing like humans. I don't know if it's because we always disliked chemicals, so used less, or if we have fewer bacteria. Maybe it's the nitrogen."

And it's weird again. People can just have keen senses.

Tia sighed loudly, indicating her annoyance with the human distinction.

"Anyway, I was thrilled when I met Nafasi and Sebastian and the others. Just to talk about things and not have to hide was—and is—a huge relief."

"What about the fashionistas? Do you think all those pretty people are close friends now? Date each other? Or just experiencing the same sense of relief as you?" Tia asked.

"I don't know. The people I have brought here, to Nafasi, have been generally very wealthy. Like

Naf, some got their money because they come from wealthy families. Some used their special skills to make them rich. Generally, they have been nervous and reserved at first. I pitch Nafasi as a genius spiritual leader and that lures them in. They meet Naf and love it here. They travel with him. Take assignments. Get involved. They stick together; they are guests, not staff. I'm not here often, usually out tracking. This is the longest I have stayed at the Hotel Center at one time. When I do see them, like at the pool party, they say 'hi' and are nice, but that is about it for conversation. Sometimes, I get a 'thank you' for convincing them to come here," Ian explained. "But that's it. I haven't had a deep conversation with any of them. Only you."

"Has anyone else thought this was bullshit?' Tia asked.

Ian turned to Tia, putting his hands on her arms to make her stop and look at him.

"You still don't accept what you are? After all you have seen and heard?" Ian asked.

"I don't know. I can excuse everything I have seen as the work of mad scientists, egomaniacal cult leaders, rich, beautiful people struggling to deal with the shooting, and cute young guys finding themselves after difficult childhoods. Maybe the young guys are acting like it's all true because it's an interesting job that pays well," Tia said, shrugging dramatically.

Bullets ricocheted through the forest.

Tia and Ian ducked to the ground.

"What the fuck?" Ian said. "It's coming from near the building."

They looked at each other. "Ekstra," they said in unison.

Thirty-Four

Tia and Ian quietly returned to the building, crouching low, dodging between trees. When they were close enough to see people on the ground, Tia gasped in horror. "Are they dead?" she whispered to Ian.

"I don't know. They aren't moving," Ian whispered, his eyes huge. "Did Jordisk kill them? What the fuck?"

Tia stared at the carnage near the front door. General White, from Space Force, was lying on the ground. At least one of the SWAT cops was also on the ground. She watched as Jordisk's security team, the guys with matching perfect beards, walked into the clearing carrying two bodies dressed in black SWAT uniforms. One had no helmet and her head hung limply over the man's arms, her jet-black hair bobbing up and down with each step.

Now Tia would never know about her eyes.

Another man walked out of the woods and into the clearing. Tia thought she had seen him before in the safe room after Nafasi was shot. Three AR-15s were slung over his arms.

"That's Adam. Did he shoot them?" Ian whispered. "I always thought he was pretty cool. What the hell is going on?"

"I don't see any blood. None. Do you?" Tia asked. "Look, I think that body, closest to us, is breathing."

Then Sebastian and Ekstra walked out of the building, their eyes taking in the shocking scene.

"What the hell, Adam?" Jordisk shouted as he entered the clearing and ran toward the building. "People can hear that for miles! Now we will have more people snooping around!"

"I'm sorry! I was just carrying them up from the truck and it went off!" Adam replied. "I'm so sorry!"

"It just went off?" Jordisk asked, sounding incredulous.

"Okay, I picked one up, like this," Adam demonstrated, pointing the gun into the woods, "just to take a look, and somehow released the safety. It's super sensitive. I've never held an assault weapon before. I've never touched a gun before. I'm sorry, Mr. Jordisk!"

"Give them to me before you kill someone—or yourself," Jordisk said, reaching for the weapons. "We'll lock them up and destroy them with the laser as soon as this is over. Well, if we are still here."

"Look at this, Mr. Jordisk," the man carrying the female SWAT cop said. He laid the body on the ground and used his fingers to open her eye.

"I knew it! I knew it! My source was right! One of us, a black eye, infiltrated the government! I've caught glimpses of those eyes on perimeter searches! I wonder whose side she's on?" Jordisk was so pleased, he clapped his hands together.

Sebastian walked around the body to get a closer look. "She looks a little like Tia. I guess this means Tia is not the spy, so you can stop trying to kill her."

"Maybe, I still don't trust her. I mean, we still don't know who killed Nafasi." Jordisk's attention was drawn to one of the incapacitated men, who was coughing. "Quick, put them in the basement before they wake up. Put them in different rooms. They'll just have to stay with us until after the 14th. But bring her upstairs and lock her in a bedroom. She is one of us. She might just be innocent, being used by the government. We will find out."

"Thank God they're not dead!" Tia whispered to Ian.

A sudden movement near her foot caught her eye. "Where the hell have you been? I was worried! You okay?" Tia asked the cat. Clorox looked up at Tia with her droll, confident, green eyes.

"What do we do now?" Ian asked. "We have the cat. Maybe we should just leave?"

"Sounds good to me," Tia said, before realizing the cat was gone. "Wait, where did she go? Dammit, Clorox!"

Tia and Ian turned to look for her and jumped.

Mr. Jordisk was leaning against a tree, coolly watching them. "You're not going anywhere."

Thirty-Five

"I'm not going back in that building, or to the Hotel Center, or *anywhere* with you," Tia said.

"I need Ian's help, and possibly yours as well, Tia. We have just over twenty-four hours left. We don't have any time to waste. More people may come because of Adam's mistake," Jordisk said calmly.

"I don't care. I'm outta here. Besides, since you are still 'not sure' if I had something to do with Nafasi's murder, you should be happy I'm leaving. One less psychopath to worry about," Tia said. "When all those government people are reported missing, more will come, so you can't just blame Adam."

I hate this fucker. Of course, he blames his subordinates. Alien or human, he is a natural asshole.

"I could come over there and incapacitate you so fast you would have no idea what happened. I could do anything I want to you. You have not seen my full potential—or anyone else's. You have no idea what you are capable of. Are you really going to return to hiding to blend in with humans? A pathetic, weak, pointless life of seeking out nature and solitude like an animal. Soon, we will all know who we really are, where we come from, and hopefully, leave this place forever. No one will impede our work—not you, nor the mewling, feeble government," Jordisk said, walking slowly toward them.

He shifted into a white blob, except for his mouth which became a black hole. Heat radiated from him, reminding Tia of the sensation when her whole body felt like it was on fire.

She turned and ran as fast as she could. She flew through the woods, dodging trees, and jumping over logs, not looking back.

She ran smack into Jordisk.

"Stupid girl, now Ian will have to carry you back up this hill," Jordisk said, leaning in like he was going to kiss her. It was the last thing Tia remembered.

When Tia groggily woke up, her head hurt and she felt nauseous. It hurt to even try to open her eyes.

What did that fucker do to me?

Ian, who was carrying her over his shoulder, must have sensed that she was stirring. He whispered, "Stop Tia, just act asleep. We're close to the building. He's just up there and can circle back and kill you. Pretend you're out, for your own good. Okay?"

Fuck! I don't want to return to that building!

Tia opened her eyes a crack. She hoped it would stop her from puking. Either dangling over Ian's shoulder or whatever Jordisk did to her—or maybe, a combination of the two—was making her want to gag. She was happy she opened her eyes because she caught a glimpse of gray and white fur hustling between the trees.

Thank God Clorox is free. She must be okay because she is moving fast.

Tia exhaled a loud sigh of relief and closed her eyes again. Opening them had not settled her stomach and gave her a piercing headache. She was extremely uncomfortable. It dawned on her that Ian was remarkably strong. He was moving silently, not even panting. His arm muscles tensed around her waist when he readjusted her. She was tall and muscular, and he was carrying her like she was just a sack of potatoes flung over his shoulder. It was terribly hot in the forest, but he wasn't even sweating.

He must be an alien. I'm hot and sweaty and my head is killing me. I feel like puking and I want down. Maybe I am just a human.

Tia opened her eyes again to see if she could tell where she was. She had run in a panic, trying to put as much distance between herself and Jordisk. Now, she was being punished for it. Tia tensed up when she caught another unnatural movement in the forest. Clorox had ducked under a pine tree, so it was not her. The color was bright white, not a bear or tiger. It looked like a jacket, like a white jacket. And is that pink? Tia squinted and could make out a shape. It looked like a human. Was there a person in the woods, watching Tia being carried up the hill?

What the hell? Who is that? Where is my awesome super alien vision when I need it?

Tia lost sight of whatever it was as they moved through the trees; the heat of the sun hit her when they moved out of the forest and into the clearing.

"Put her in the room with the other black-eyed woman. They should talk," Jordisk said.

As soon as Ian passed through the door of the building, the alarm went off, making Tia jump.

"Good, Tia's awake. Lock her up and then do a perimeter check. Go all the way to the Center. Without drones or communications, we need to go old school and make sure no one else is on the property. All hands on deck," Jordisk shouted over the alarm.

"Got it," Ian replied.

"Room 11," Sebastian said. "Take Tia there and then go."

"I can walk," Tia said.

"Shush," Ian whispered, carrying her down a hall and stopping in front of a door. He slid her down his body to gently place her on the ground. "Just stay here. I'll be back soon."

Thirty-Six

Ian locked the door from the outside. Tia rolled her eyes dramatically at the woman to show her how annoyed she was by the situation. "Hi," Tia said.

The woman just stared at her; her head cocked.

She was on the bed, leaning back against the pillows with her legs stretched out in front of her. Her dirty boots were on the comforter. The room was larger than the one Tia stayed in the night before, but not by much; there was just enough space for two twin beds, a table and chair, and a large mirror that made the room appear larger. A small table between the beds had a lamp with a pink and purple shade; it looked like it belonged in a children's room.

Tia went and used the tiny bathroom. She splashed cold water on her face and looked at her reflection. They had the same eyes, that was for sure. Similar hair as well.

I'm not as freaked out as I was when I first saw her eyes. I will just be cool. See what she knows.

Tia left the bathroom and flopped down on the other bed. "So, do you have aniridia or are you an extraterrestrial?" Tia asked.

The woman just stared at her.

"Okay, you don't have to answer, but there is some crazy ass shit happening here," Tia said. "I plan to break out soon and make a run for it. I think I will take a nap first. This has been a long and horrible day for me and my head hurts because that freak knocked me out. What about you? What is your plan?"

Tia put her head on the pillow and closed her eyes. Both to get a little rest and to avoid looking at her eyes on someone else's face.

"I tell people I have aniridia, an eye disorder, but I think I'm an alien," the woman said in a strong accent. "I have suspected it since Rex and The Pledge."

So, she thinks she's one of them. One of us?

What is that accent? Russian? Eastern European?

"Do you think there are lots of aliens among us?" Tia asked, her eyes still closed.

"No, not really. They all seem to be with Nafasi Genny. He's methodical at collecting extraterrestrials. But I guess there could be others in the world," the woman responded. "Have you noticed that most of his staff and guests look peculiar? Even if they don't have black eyes like us."

"Yes, I have noticed that. My name is Tia. I'm from Georgia—the state, not the country. I got caught up in this nightmare on a quest to find an abandoned hotel on a hill with spectacular gardens and a stunning view," Tia explained.

"Vanze Malski, from Poland. Americans often call me Van, and it is very beautiful here. I was dazzled—seriously distracted—by the many shades of green, the fresh smells, and the wildlife. I think I may have spotted a tiger before that thing came at me and knocked me out. Took my gun. Disarmed my team. I have no idea what happened to the general and the others. I should be humiliated; I'm the leader of the security team, but honestly, I'm seriously out of practice. I have not been attacked or fired a gun in five years. He did something that made me unconscious, but I don't feel a bump on my head or have any bruises. I assume it was the same prick that knocked you out, right? Do you know what he did? It's fascinating. I wonder what kind of alien he is," Van said.

"You guys are lucky. He almost killed me when I arrived. Luckily, he is using a kinder tactic today. I saw your team. They're all alive. They are being detained in the basement. I haven't been down there. It could be a jail, a torture chamber, a place for experiments, or just more small rooms, like this one. I don't know. Are the others on your security team like you?" Tia asked.

"No. None of them. The people on my security team have no idea what is happening. Most of the leadership team doesn't either. They just think I'm strange. Before Rex came, I just thought I was strange too. But after the mass shooting, I started questioning everything. I'm so excited about what I think is happening here. They are calling the others, or other extraterrestrials, right?" Van asked.

"If White and the others don't know what is happening here, then why are they here?" Tia asked, ignoring Van's question.

"I mean, they know the mission: to be on the lookout for more aliens that may have come to Earth. General White put the team together after the mass shooting and cloud message. Space Force realized there are extraterrestrials on Earth and they aren't gentle and kind—they're vastly more intelligent and vastly more violent. When I heard about the team, I volunteered. I wanted to know what was going on, and maybe learn more about myself, and my quirks. They think I have aniridia syndrome and I'm strong and very engaged and curious, which may be abnormal for a simple military security team lead. I think General White is suspicious of me sometimes," Van explained. "But he doesn't know."

She seems very open, maybe because she's so happy to know she is not alone. I hope she is telling the truth.

"You haven't fired a gun in five years?" Tia asked.

"Not since before the mass shooting," Van replied.

"Do you only eat once a day?" Tia asked.

"Preferably, yes. Sometimes I try to stretch it out to avoid calling attention to my lack of appetite. Can you easily bench your weight?" Van asked.

"Yes, and I can jump far and run fast. Not comic book strong and fast though. My hearing and sight are good; my sense of smell is pretty good, compared to most. I know that sounds terrible, but the good smells outweigh the bad," Tia replied.

"Not all the time. If you were in the military, you might think otherwise," Van said.

"I knew as a young kid I was different. People just walked past flowers, sunsets, clouds, and birds like they were not there. They didn't see the beauty. Or I would inhale deeply and say, 'Smell that moss, it smells so good' and people would say, 'What are you smelling?' I knew I was different. Of course, our eyes are unique." Tia still couldn't bring herself to open her eyes.

"Ha, unique, that is a good word for them. I was teased a lot as a kid and in basic training, but since the shooting and The Pledge, people have been a lot kinder and more considerate of people's disabilities or 'uniqueness,'" Van said. "Have you seen anyone else with eyes like ours?"

"No one I have talked to has them. But there are lots of sunglasses, so maybe," Tia said.

Memories flashed through her mind of the party and the safe room. Some had odd eyes, but not exactly like theirs.

"Shoot, if I saw someone with eyes like ours, I would speak to them immediately," Van said.

"Wait, you saw my eyes at the Center, near the porch, when you were talking to Nafasi and Wai. You looked right at me. You had on a helmet. You could see my eyes, but I couldn't see yours. I didn't see your eyes until you were walking into the woods, heading back to the Center. Did you take off your helmet on purpose so I would see?" Tia asked.

"I was playing it cool. We were in a highly charged situation amongst possible hostile aliens. I was shocked to see your eyes. I wasn't sure what to do. I mean, if I saw someone with eyes like mine at a meditation center or yoga class, I would ask them about them. What exactly is this place? A hotel? A research center? A cult?" Van asked.

"When I think of the medical rooms and this research building, I think of this place as a Center. But when I see the guests at a party or at the pool or on the schedule for yoga sessions, I think of it as a hotel. Of course, combine it all and it seems like a cult. It's a confusing place. Now that I think about it, it's also a jail," Tia said.

"Were you in Georgia the day of the mass shooting?" Van asked.

"Yes, happy I did not have a gun. Were you in Poland?" Tia asked.

"No, that day I was in Bosnia. I was already an American citizen and in the military. I did not have a gun with me on that day. If I had been here, in America, I would probably be dead. Bosnia lost 500,000 people within fifteen minutes. Chaos. Poland lost almost a million. All nations were devastated, whether a country lost 5,000 or like China, 50,000,000. It changed everything. The dynamics of geopolitical hostility changed too, for the better. Some nations had more private gun ownership and some more military arms. It's a good thing Rex did not seem to understand military gun ownership, or things may have been worse. But don't worry, America still has a military, just not an armed one," Van explained.

"Except for you and your team. Why do we even need a military?" Tia sighed loudly. "Oh, never mind, I don't care."

"Do you think it's possible we are from the same place, the same planet? Are we the same species?" Van asked.

"I have no idea," Tia replied.

I'm not sure I'm willing to admit or accept I'm anything other than a strange human.

"Why do our eyes look like this? Does Mr. Genny or any of the others know?" Van asked.

"I don't know, maybe it's the extra nitrogen?" Tia wondered out loud.

"What extra nitrogen?" Van asked.

"Huh, Nafasi never saw your eyes? Or explained the situation to you?" Tia asked.

"No, I never let him see my eyes. I was only in his presence a few times, just listening and guarding General White. I didn't hear anything about nitrogen. We do know Genny is using a powerful telescope to shoot electromagnetic beams into outer space. He seemed to have learned how to do so in Hawaii and West Virginia, refined the technology in other countries, and then created or built this beast of a machine here. We think he bought or stole some of the technology collected in Florida. You know, from that collision six years ago that killed Rex's people and brought on the mass shooting. We have been watching him and the Center for two years. I do perimeter sweeps a few nights a month and inform White of what I see," Van explained.

I bet Jordisk has seen her and her eyes while he does his super-fast security sweeps! That is why he confused us and tried to kill me.

"Maybe Nafasi found his nitrogen detector technology in the collision debris. I haven't seen it, just heard about it," Tia said.

"General White has talked to Genny a few times. White told him he needed permits, and to work with the government and that he must explain what he is doing. Genny just acts like a rich cult leader with vague responses like, 'I'm looking for answers in space.' He says he is on a, 'Quest for peace, both internal and external.' White thinks he is nuts but is worried about the powerful telescope and laser. White always worries about rich arrogant bros messing things up in space. He has straight up asked me if I think Genny is trying to communicate with aliens," Van continued.

"What do you say?" Tia asked, sitting up and looking into Van's eyes that mirrored her own.

"That Genny is a rich, spoiled, and arrogant man, but I can't imagine he would be able to talk to extraterrestrials. I remind him that when Kate and Sinclair worked with Rex, they didn't initiate the conversation," Van responded. "I tell him that Genny is delusional."

"But what do you think?"

"I think Genny is trying to communicate with the others. I hope so. I would love to find out what I am, where I came from, maybe go explore space and find my home," Van said wistfully. "I guess find *our* home."

"So, you're playing both sides: observing what is happening to fulfill your curiosity but telling White he is being paranoid and there is nothing to see here," Tia said.

"Yes," Van replied. "But think about it: what can General White do? Whether Genny is calling aliens or is a delusional cult leader, what can White do about it? Go all Waco Texas on their asses? It would violate The Pledge. We aren't even supposed to have weapons. And Genny is very charming; he seems to calm White down every time they talk. Except they have been shooting that beam up a lot this month, and with the anniversary of July 14 quickly approaching,

White had to get more serious and ask hard questions and demand to see the equipment." Van laid back and looked at the ceiling. "And White was at Kennedy Space Center when Kate, Sinclair, and Rex destroyed the debris. Hell, we all know how powerful Rex and the others are. Even if Genny is calling them to come back, what can White do to stop it?"

"Is that why White had someone shoot Nafasi?" Tia asked, watching Van closely to see how she responded.

"Shit, is Genny dead?" Van asked, snapping up into a seated position and slamming her boots on the floor. "How? Who? Why? Shit, *when*? And they are still shooting that laser into space? Who's in charge now?"

Tia put her feet on the floor and leaned close to Van's face, looking into her eyes. Van stared back.

Tia shrugged.

If neither Van nor the government shot him, who killed Nafasi?

Suddenly, the alarm blared.

Damn, I thought they were lowering the volume. It's making my head hurt worse.

The solar flares had knocked out the power and communications, a good time to use the laser again; no one would see what was happening.

Has the government made that connection yet?

Van jumped at the noise. "What is that sound? What does it mean?" she shouted.

I guess that answers that question. Van hasn't made the connection. Of course, that doesn't necessarily mean White hasn't. If White suspects Van might be an 'other,' perhaps he doesn't entirely trust her. Except, he did trust her with guns.

"How do you justify using a gun? I mean, after the mass shooting and The Pledge, how do you justify it to yourself? They aren't safe for anyone and now your weapons are in the hands of the people that locked us up. Does The Pledge mean nothing to you?" Tia asked, shouting in frustration and to be heard over the alarm.

Van laughed. "*Please.* People say one thing and do another all the time. I wasn't sure I was an alien when I signed it, though I knew I wanted to go into space. I hoped Rex would take us with him and was disappointed when nothing happened. Like I said, I haven't owned or fired a weapon since the shooting and White got scared about what was happening here. I guess fear and guns just go together."

"It was nice meeting you, Van, but I need to go," Tia yelled.

She jumped up, and kicked the door hard, knocking it off its hinges. She rushed down the hall.

Van doesn't understand the reason for the alarm. With Ekstra and his staff obsessed with the anniversary closing in, and Jordisk's security people searching the property with Ian, this is my opportunity to finally hit the road.

Thirty-seven

Tia opened the main door to the building and quickly ran outside.

I'm free.

Jordisk grabbed her roughly by her hair.

"Fuck! Let me go!" Tia screamed in frustration.

"What did she say? The black-eyed soldier? Did she kill Nafasi? I figured you two bonded. Must be amazing to meet someone of your species. I would love that. I mean, that is why we're doing all this," he said, directing her back toward the building. "You are extremely lucky."

I don't feel lucky.

"Get your hands off me!" Tia shouted.

"Tell me what she said or I'll burn you alive. Then I'll kill Ian for being annoying—maybe Sebastian too. I need Ekstra and his brain so he'll be safe," Jordisk said, pulling her face so close to his that she could feel the heat, and see the black hole forming. Everything smelled like fire.

"Her name is Van. She thinks she is an alien. She doesn't think General White or his colleagues know, though she thinks they must be suspicious. They know about the laser and are worried it's being used to call Rex and the others. She was shocked to hear

Nafasi is dead. She didn't kill him. She doesn't think White did either. I'm not sure about the other government people. Maybe someone shot him without her knowing? But, based on her answer, emotional response, and my gut, I don't think the government killed Nafasi," Tia said, looking away from his glowing white skin and terrifying gaping mouth.

Jordisk pushed her away and stared up at the sky for a couple of seconds, inhaling deeply. "Okay then." He grabbed Tia by the arm so hard that her feet came off the ground.

Tia screamed in fear, but he just dragged her down a hall.

"You must realize it was not me spying on you! It was Van!" Tia yelled.

Jordisk stopped in front of a door, opened it, and shoved Tia into the small room.

He followed her in and grabbed her head from behind, forcing her face against his. "If you break this lock or door, I will kill Ian. If I can't find that soldier bitch, I will kill Ian. If you are not here when I return, I will kill Ian," Jordisk said.

Tia screamed as his mouth turned into a black swirling hole that smelled acrid.

⊕

Tia jerked awake. All was silent.

She was lying on a small cot. It didn't have a sheet or blanket. The room smelled odd, like sulfur dioxide. There was a desk, chair, and glaring overhead light, but nothing else in the room. There was a slightly ajar door so close to the cot that she could touch it, leading to a tiny bathroom. The room seemed more like a large closet. She got up and, holding her head, walked to the door. She tried the doorknob, but it was locked. She jiggled it and heard a click. She could easily snap it off and walk out.

For a building full of the most modern tech, these locks are so old-fashioned. Does someone have keys? They are so flimsy; I have never actually been locked in anywhere. But there has almost always been someone in the hall, just outside the door.

"Hello? Is anyone out there? Ian? Sebastian?" Tia called through the door. No one responded.

The pain of the headache made her pant and she tried to slow her breathing to heal. Her arms were red and angry from Jordisk's grip; some of the finger-shaped marks were already turning into ugly bruises. She felt around and decided nothing was broken. It took a lot to break her bones, but Jordisk was incredibly strong. If anyone could, it would be him.

The room made her feel claustrophobic. She sat down in the chair and put her head in her hands. The alarm went off.

Fuck! Okay, this room isn't soundproof. I wish it was soundproof! My head is going to explode! Why are they still using the alarm? I wonder if anything out there has seen the beam yet. I mean, the alarm is so fucking loud they must hear it on Saturn! Why can't they just turn it off once they get the telescope going?

Tia took deep breaths, trying to block out the noise. The alarm went on and on and on.

This one is long. Come to think of it, do they keep getting longer? The first ones were just a few minutes. I wonder if something has gone wrong. I hope Ekstra is okay. Should I smash down the door and go check on him?

Tia laid back on the cot and rubbed her arms gently to stimulate blood flow and help the healing, trying to take her mind off the painful noise.

Jordisk must have knocked me out like White, Van, and the other government people. But Van seemed fine when they put me in the room with her. Maybe he used a lower dosage of burning poison gas on her? Or maybe she heals faster, and we aren't the same kind of alien after all? Of course, they don't have modern locks here. I guess it would not be good if Ekstra or the other scientists got locked in their rooms when the power went out and the alarms went off. Especially this little windowless closet room. A normal, healthy person could go mad here. Clorox would hate it in here. I do hope she is okay. She looked okay earlier when Ian was carrying me. What time is it? I think this noise is going to drive me insane!

The alarm stopped.

Thank God. One more minute and I would've broken down the door, even if it caused Ian's murder. I think something is wrong with me. I have such a headache…

Thirty-Eight

Tia jerked awake, listening for the alarm. It was silent. She studied her arms. They were much better, and her head did not hurt.

She got up and used the tiny bathroom. She splashed water on her face and rinsed out her mouth.

How long have I been asleep? How long have I been in this room? I look like hell. Of course, my hair looks the same as always. Just like Van's. What's up with that? We discussed the eyes but not the hair. I wonder if everyone on our planet looks similar and like us. Or maybe we are just one species on the planet that looks the same, like deer or cockroaches? Either way, how boring. Do the males and females all look alike? Are there males and females? I wonder if there are any cute boys like Ian? Fuck, did I just say, 'our planet'?

Tia jumped at a loud pounding on the other side of the door.

"Tia, let's go. Come out," Ian shouted through the door.

Tia flung the door wide and jumped into his arms. "I'm so happy you're alive! And that you look different from me!" Tia said, laughing.

"That's great, but no time for games. All hell has broken loose. Wait, let's go back inside, we need to talk," Ian said, taking Tia's hand and walking back into the tiny room. He shut the door.

"I was doing security perimeter checks, but without drones, we were running blind all night. It also rained, making it harder to see. The woods between here and the hotel are dense, as you know. When the sun finally came out, there were soldiers and government types everywhere, I guess they came looking for General White and his colleagues."

"What time is it?" Tia asked.

"Around 11 o'clock," Ian replied.

"Fuck, I've been in here for almost twenty-four hours! No wonder I was going insane. What did he do to me?" Tia asked.

"I don't know, Tia, but things are bad. As it got lighter, Jordisk was infuriated that so many humans were roaming around on the property, especially on the anniversary. He said he would take care of it. Me, Sebastian, and Jordisk's security team tried to talk him out of it. We said, 'Hey, just keep using the laser continuously.' I mean, the cat is clearly out of the bag. Just stay in the building until the others respond or arrive. Ignore the humans. They can't do anything to stop us now. The guests and staff are hunkered down and safe at the hotel. Just get through this day, release the prisoners, apologize to the government, and we all move forward," Ian explained.

"That's a great idea. I mean, technically the rapture would happen or not happen, regardless of the human's investigation. I mean, aliens can do whatever they want whenever they want," Tia said. "Jordisk, you, and all the aliens can go to space and just leave us alone."

"Wait, do you still not believe you are one of us or are you joking? Because none of this is funny," Ian said.

"Let's just get out of here!" Tia said, exasperated.

"Fine, but we need to be very careful. I don't want to be shot by a soldier or burned alive by Jordisk," Ian said, leading Tia out of the room and building.

As they were about to walk out the main door, one of the older bearded gentlemen from Jordisk's security team walked in.

"I wouldn't go out there, Ian. It's safer in here. Total shitshow out there," he said, giving Tia a nod.

"We need to leave," Tia replied.

"Okay. It's your life," he responded.

"Wait, do either of you know where the woman with eyes like mine is? The soldier in all black?" Tia asked.

"I haven't seen her since she was unconscious on the ground outside," Ian said, pointing at the door.

"Most of the government people are still locked in the basement. She's upstairs with Ekstra and his team. Jordisk gave the okay. I guess he trusts her now," the bearded security man said.

The alarm went off again.

"Stay in here. Go upstairs. It's safer. A few of the guests came here and are upstairs, waiting with champagne. We are so close to noon." The security guy walked away, heading toward the elevator.

Ian grabbed Tia's hand and they ran out the door, through the grassy clearing, and into the forest. They ran for several minutes before Tia stepped on something that did not feel right. She whipped around to see what had almost tripped her. It was a body.

"Oh my God!" Tia cried, putting her hands to her mouth in horror.

It was one of the generals.

"Did Jordisk kill him?" Tia exclaimed.

"Don't know," Ian said, turning him over. "Hmmm, doesn't look like Jordisk's work. He is all bruises and burning and carbon monoxide to make people pass out. This man is dead."

Tia bent down for a better look. "Oh my God, there are bullet holes," Tia said when she noticed the tiny round holes in his suit near his stomach. "Almost no blood. Remember how we learned from all those mass shootings at movie theaters, schools, and churches that assault weapons can disintegrate organs? Fuck. Who is doing the shooting? The same person that shot Nafasi?"

"I don't know, but we gotta get out of here," Ian said, taking her hand.

"Shit! Another body." Tia pointed a hundred feet away.

When they got close, they saw a bullet hole in the soldier's forehead.

Suddenly the alarm stopped. While the silence would normally be appreciated, it made Tia feel more exposed. Anyone could hear them. They started moving again, fast and quiet, bobbing and weaving between the trees.

As they entered another clearing, Tia gasped in horror. Sprinkled around were several dead bodies, all smoldering. "*This* is Jordisk's work," Tia said.

Clorox appeared in the clearing. She looked directly at Tia. Tia could see distress in her eyes, almost as bad as when she found her in the woods near the road that led to town.

"What's wrong, Clorox? Are you in pain?" Tia called to her.

Clorox took off running and Tia chased after her, Ian following close behind.

After they had been running for several minutes, Ian grabbed Tia's arm and swung her around. "Tia, she's leading you back to the building! Back to danger! Are you sure you want to follow her?"

Tia hesitated briefly and took a deep breath. She looked Ian in the eyes. "Yes, I need to follow her. I don't know why. Just like I don't know why I run faster or jump higher or lift more than most. Or why I think everything is so beautiful. Or honestly, why do I keep denying everything you said when it was crystal clear you were right? Thank you for showing me the truth," Tia said before she leaned in and kissed him.

Her body flushed hot as blood rushed through her veins. She could hear both of their hearts. It was an intense kiss and Tia was breathless when she pulled away.

"I have to go and see what she needs," Tia said. "Keep going. Get out of this deadly place, Ian."

"Nope, I'm coming with you. I didn't think I would ever meet anyone who appreciates nature and sunsets as much as I do. I didn't think I would ever meet anyone that makes me feel so alive and comfortable. No one so much like me," Ian said, smiling.

"Because we're from another planet?" Tia asked, finally able to admit what she was.

"No, because we survived the foster system!" Ian laughed. "Now let's go find your damn cat!"

Thirty-Nine

As they followed Clorox, the alarm started again. Tia's head hurt; she put her hands over her ears to block out the noise.

Clorox ran out of the forest, across the clearing, and directly to the door. She paused and looked at it, waiting for Tia to catch up and open it.

Tia ran across the clearing, just as the door swung open. One of the soldiers dressed in SWAT gear stumbled out of the building. There was blood on his face, and he was holding his chest as though he had been shot. He looked at Tia before he fell.

Tia came to a screeching halt and lost her balance, sliding down on her ass.

The alarm stopped.

Ian caught up to Tia, "Fuck the cat. She led us straight to the killers!"

The door was still open, and a woman walked through it and stepped over the soldier's body without looking at it. She wore white shorts, a pink tank top, old-school Converse sneakers, and 1950s Ray-Ban sunglasses. Her long blond hair was loose and hung down to her waist.

The DJ from the sunset party.

She was carrying a large black handgun.

General White came running out of the building behind her. He looked at the soldier in horror and then at the woman.

"Why did you let us out just to shoot him?" White demanded, looking incredulous.

"You need to leave this place. That is what I told you to do, not come after me. There is no time, it's almost noon. Now, you can continue to bullshit with me, or you can get the hell out of here," she replied.

White looked confused. "Someone needs to stop this madness! They're calling Rex and the others!"

"Don't worry about it. I've got this. Seriously, I've got this. Just leave. It's for the best," the DJ said.

White glanced at Tia, who was still on the ground, and Ian, standing close by, before he turned and walked back into the building.

"Damn, men just refuse to listen to women," the DJ said, watching the door close. She turned and walked slowly toward Tia and Ian, pointing the handgun at them. "These are so much more elegant than assault weapons and easier to use. Though, they both serve their purpose."

"You're the DJ, right?" Tia asked, her voice shaking in fear and disbelief.

"I brought you here. I found you in LA and brought you to Nafasi three years ago. Tia, this is one of the wealthy people I tracked and brought here. She rarely talks to me. An occasional hello or asks me what I want to listen to at the parties. What's going on Jules? Did you shoot that guy? Why?" Ian demanded as he helped Tia to her feet.

"Why? Why?! I like it here! When you first brought me to Nafasi, I was open-minded. It was great to finally understand what I was. Like everyone, I knew I was peculiar. But then I got to thinking, why was I dropped here? Were there many others besides us? Sure, **Naf** has a nice collection and there probably are more of us on Earth, but not that many; we are kind of special. For whatever reason, we are here, and we survived. We adapted. Hell, we *thrived*. We can breathe the air and swim in the oceans and eat and maybe, we can evolve. I love the music here—all of it, all kinds. I love whales and dolphins and walking on the beach. I love watching sunsets all over the world." Jules laughed with glee and spun around with her hands outstretched like she was listening to music, whipping the gun around.

Tia and Ian just stared at her.

"This planet is amazing and since The Pledge, it has only gotten better," Jules said, dancing. "People are kind. People have cleaned up pollution and stopped creating more. Nature has rebounded. This is fucking paradise!"

But then she stopped dancing. She fiddled with the gun. "But then Nafasi casually decided to invite extra-terrestrials to Earth. Or back to Earth, in the case of Rex and his kind. This rich, self-centered, spoiled rotten egomaniac made this enormously important decision for all of us. What does he want? To fill some empty hole in himself? He put us—humans, nature, wildlife, and Earth—in great danger for his selfish fun. Hells to the fucking *no!*"

"You can't know for sure that they will hurt anyone this time. You can't be angry with Nafasi for making decisions for others if you are kind of doing the same, right?" Ian asked.

"I guess I am, but I also listened carefully. When we are at parties, on Naf's yacht, flying to Hawaii, or just having dinner at the Hotel Center, I would pay attention. I would hear people and staff ask questions, and express concerns, but Nafasi would blow them off," Jules said. "I would talk to them. I asked them if they thought this world was good. If they wanted to live here in peace. If they thought this planet and life were worth fighting for, and some agreed. I'm not alone. We know it's worth protecting, even if we had to kill that dumbass, rich, arrogant, megalomaniac to do so."

Fuck. She killed Nafasi!

"Look, you two have a choice. You can go in there with Ekstra and Sebastian and the others and wait for God knows what to arrive and take you God knows where. Maybe your home planet? Maybe they'll like it here, on Earth, and decide to stay. Maybe they'll work together and take over this world."

She stared hard at Tia and Ian.

"But please remember, Rex and the others were violent psychopaths. Rex killed hundreds of millions of people. I mean, what was Nafasi's real plan? Did he think he could work with 'the others?' Total madness," Jules said.

Tia and Ian just stared at her in shock. Clorox walked a few feet away from the DJ, sat down, and started to bathe herself.

"Or you can go in there and join General White and what is left of his staff," Jules continued, pointing the gun at the dead body. "You can try to turn off the laser and save the world. However, I don't think Ekstra will let that happen. The government was not behaving rationally either; they were reverting to the pointless, stupid thinking from before the shooting. They tried to use secrecy, lies, intimidation, and finally, guns to solve a huge, complicated problem. Totally violating The Pledge. It might not be the laser beam invitation that brings Rex back to Earth but their behavior."

Tia hoped Ian would not point out the Jules's hypocrisy again and risk pissing her off.

Jules shook her head with disgust and glanced up at the sky. "Van is with them, upstairs with the telescope. I kind of wondered what way she would go since she works for the government. I have been watching her for some time. I've been monitoring this whole fucked up game since 2022. I allowed Ian to bring me here to get closer to Nafasi. I knew that, for the past year, Van had been roaming around the property, spying. She was fast, sneaky, and extraordinary as both a well-trained soldier and an alien. Jordisk would catch glimpses of her but could never catch her. He became obsessed and frustrated. He knew it was a fast woman with black eyes, and then you just casually walked up his hill. He was convinced you were the spy. You weakened Jordisk by distracting him. It was helpful. Now, Van is up there with her fellow aliens, all giddy with excitement that she might be going home. She's stupid." Jules sighed.

"So Jordisk should love her now. They are on the same team, right?" Tia asked.

Jules shrugged dramatically. "It was stupid of Jordisk to lock up White and his staff. When they went missing, Space Force and the DoD sent more soldiers. So much unnecessary violence. Anyway, your choice. I'm out of here."

What the fuck? She is also a spy, liar, killer, and playing all sides! Are all aliens fucking nuts?

"Where is Jordisk? Like you, he seemed to have killed a lot of people last night," Ian said.

"I killed Jordisk. Shot him in the head with an AR-15. I was not entirely sure he would die, what with all his creepy powers. That mouth? Those poisonous burning things he could produce? Wow, he came from a violent planet, that's for sure. I could see him starting some intergalactic war, or just setting us back to pre-shooting days with endless wars, horrific pollution, and greed. People would feel helpless again, unable to solve even the simplest problem. He needed to die. He's been losing his shit ever since I shot Nafasi," Jules said, swaying again like she could hear music.

"Wait, you haven't even really given us a choice. Go inside that building and join forces with assholes on whichever side we choose? *That* is the choice we get to make?" Tia asked.

"Oh right, or you stay out here. That is the other choice. Stay out here on this gorgeous planet—the best planet in the solar system and the universe. Stay out here in nature that is full of animals and plants and lakes and oceans and fluffy *natural* clouds and amazing sunsets. Stay out here in a world that has embraced a truly sustainable way of life that is fair and equitable to all. Not to mention, values kindness and love above everything for everything. That is your choice. You'd better make it fast, it's almost noon," Jules said, glancing at her watch.

Tia and Ian looked at each other.

"She's crazy," Tia mouthed.

Jules bent down and rubbed Clorox on the head and back. The cat leaned into the pets.

"She's gorgeous. Her nitrogen levels are off the charts, just like yours, Tia. So strange. Maybe she did come with you? But that would mean planning, maybe not just a random accident. What do you think, kitty? Do you know something? You're a good kitty, very good at looking after Tia. Keep watching over her while I take care of this mess. Bye, pretty kitty." Jules smiled at the cat.

Clorox purred loudly.

"Well? What do you choose?" Jules asked, standing up.

"To stay out here," Tia and Ian said at the same time.

"Okay, bye, Ian and Tia," Jules said, heading toward the forest. Just before she walked out of the clearing, and into the woods, she looked back at them. "I've got this. I'm preventing a huge problem and cleaning up the mess." She dramatically tossed the handgun away and disappeared into the forest.

"Let's get the fuck out of here," Ian said.

"That is what I have been saying all along," Tia said, taking his hand. Together, they ran through the clearing in the opposite direction of Jules. "Maybe our mansion in Deep Creek is still available."

"Come on, Clorox, keep up!" Ian called to the cat.

They ran into the forest, slowing down when they approached the place with the dead bodies. Ian pointed dramatically at one as they passed and Tia could see it was, indeed, Tom Jordisk in his human form.

In the distance, the alarm went off again, signaling that the solar flares had shut down communication and the laser could be up and running.

Suddenly, there was an explosion so enormous it shook the ground and made Tia, Ian, and Clorox fall hard. A huge cloud was visible above the trees. Tia and Ian lay on their backs, looking up at the dark ominous cloud of smoke and debris in bewilderment. A second explosion shook the forest again, this one from farther away.

"I think the Hill View Hotel Center is no more!" Ian shouted to be heard above the noise.

They got up and started running as fast as they could.

Epilogue

Several weeks later, Tia and Ian were back at the mansion in Deep Creek, watching the sunset.

"How does it seem more spectacular every evening?" Ian asked. "Inhale deeply, you can smell the leaves starting to change colors."

"Look," Tia exclaimed, pointing at a mama bear with three cubs meandering out of the woods and toward the lake.

Startled ducks quacked loudly as they flew away from the family. Tia giggled as the babies played along the shoreline.

"I wish we never had to leave this place," Ian said. "It's been the perfect hideout, waiting for the heat to blow over."

Tia and Ian went into town once a week to catch the news on a bar TV or go online at the library to read the latest speculations about what happened at Nafasi Genny's Hill View Hotel Center. The generally accepted story was that Genny was running a dangerous cult, trying to reach Rex and the others. Space Force, the DoD, and other agencies were tracking it and when they confronted Genny, he and his security team went crazy, killing many agents and blowing up their own Center. The calls for witnesses, or anyone who had any information regarding what happened, had died down. The town of Janssen was in shock. It was the most horrible and violent news in years and had the world on edge.

Tia winced, thinking about Caitlin and her family. Caitlin had saved her life after Jordisk assaulted her. Neither they nor their small town deserved more trauma. Her heart felt icy cold when images of the doctor, Sebastian, and Ekstra flashed across her mind. The circumstances were complicated but they had been kind and taught her so much and their deaths made her sad. She shook her head to clear her thoughts.

"Now that we feel confident that they either don't know we were there or assume we died in the explosion, we need to go," Tia said.

"Okay, but where will we go?" Ian asked, looking around at their solitary paradise.

It will be hard to leave this place.

"We need to go to Florida," she replied, watching the cubs frolic.

"Why, before it gets cold?" Ian asked.

Tia laughed. "Well, that, but mostly because we need to talk to Kate Stellute and Dr. Sinclair Jones. We need to tell them what happened."

"Why?" Ian asked, taking her hand and pulling her into his lap.

Tia traced the lines on his tanned forehead. "Because, what if one of the messages was received?"

THE END

QUESTIONS AND TOPICS
FOR DISCUSSION

1. Tia and Ian were raised in the foster system. In what ways is this relevant to the story?

2. There are examples of hypocrisy throughout the story. Can you name some and elaborate on their relevance to the plot?

3. The world has significantly changed in the five years since the shooting. Can you name some examples that impact business, family, and geopolitics?

4. There are examples of different personality traits in the story, such as antisocial, narcissistic, overly aggressive, paranoid, and manipulative. Can you name the characters and behaviors that express these traits?

5. There have been numerous benefits to nature and wildlife since the shooting, can you name a few and why? What are your favorites?

6. What do you think of The Pledge? Do you think it would be difficult to adhere to it? Would it make you feel more stressed or happy?

7. Most characters have good traits and bad. Can you name some of them in Nafasi, Van, Tom Jordisk, Ekstraterès, General White, Jules, Ian, and Tia?

8. Close your eyes and envision other changes (not mentioned in the book) in a world without guns. What are they? Are they beneficial or harmful?

9. Is Tia a hero in this story? What role does she play in the outcome? Are there other heroes?

10. Has this novel motivated you to learn more about the environment and take some concrete, meaningful action?

About The Author

C K Westbrook is the author of the science fiction series, "The Impact Series." CK is an environmentalist who lives and works in Washington, D.C., and is a self-described old-school news junkie. Since the state of our planet and the news is bleak and depressing, CK escapes reality by creating intriguing characters in a science fiction world. The world these characters live in may also be dark and scary, but they have fantastic adventures that impact their planet. In addition to creating imaginative stories, CK breaks free from daily life with an intense passion for travel and has been to all seven continents. CK loves weaving real-world topics and crises into suspenseful sci-fi and fantasy. To learn more about CK Westbrook, please go to www.ckwestbrook.com and 4horsemen-publications.com, on Twitter @WestbrookCK, and as CK Westbrook Author on Facebook, Instagram, and TikTok.